Things
found during
THE Autopsy

short fiction by
KUZHALI
MANICKAVEL

BLAFT

PUBLICATIONS
PRIVATE LIMITED

Chennai

Blaft Publications Pvt. Ltd.
4/192 Ellaiamman Koil St., Neelankarai, Chennai 600041 India
http://blaft.com

ISBN 978-93-80636-17-7

Cover design by Prabha Mallya

Printed at Sudarsan Graphics

ALSO BY KUZHALI MANICKAVEL

INSECTS ARE JUST LIKE YOU AND ME EXCEPT SOME OF THEM HAVE WINGS
(SHORT FICTION)

EATING SUGAR, TELLING LIES
(E-CHAPBOOK)

Contents

The Whore Raft   1

How to Wear an Indian Village   6

The Ash Eaters   7

The Tar Heroin Guide to Melting a Snowman   8

The Twins   12

The Decline and Fall of Western Dance in a South Indian Women's College   16

This Is Us and This Is Us Outside   32

Everyone Does Integral Calculus   34

Jugni   37

The Underground Bird Sanctuary   44

The Four Steps of Standard Plastination   51

Go Home, Dallas   54

Frostbite   57

The Gods in the Basement   60

The Most Beautiful Woman in the World Is Calling Me Niggerbitch   63

How Juniper Parsnip Saved Christmas Eve   66

Pazhani   78

Boys Like That   83

Saint Diesel   87

Kisi Shayar Something Something   90

You Can't and You Don't   93

This Old Man   94

Discuss How India Will Become a Prosperous and Secure Nation
in the Next Five Years   98

Daily Future Life Predictions
from the HotMalluAuntyWetSariSexBoobs DotcomCenter
in the Tropicool Icy-Land Urban Indian Slum   101

Transcripts from Interviews
with Three Spiritual Entities Trapped Inside a Young Girl
in the Tropicool Icy-Land Urban Indian Slum   108

Three Scenarios Leading to the Rape of a Teenage Girl
in the Tropicool Icy-Land Urban Indian Slum   113

The Importance of Having a Minty-Fresh Export-Quality
Aadi Velli Special Non-Cola Cola
in the Tropicool Icy-Land Urban Indian Slum   117

A Basic Guide to Instigating Violence against Gentoo Penguins
in the Tropicool Icy-Land Urban Indian Slum   120

Whore   127

The Good Place   129

Movie People   132

The Statue Game   135

We Will All Get Better and Then We Will Get Worse   145

Shapeshifters   155

The Party House   158

When the Other Girls Come   161

Put Your Hand in the Hand of the Man with his Hand in the Hand of the Man
with his Hand in the Windmills of your Mind   163

Six Things We Found During the Autopsy   170

We Will Speak About Brain Aneurysms   173

Throwing Rocks at Dogs   175

Take a Girl and Put Her in a Natural Setting   184

firang   186

The Flood   187

Two Girls   190

Anarch   192

Things WE found during THE Autopsy

the whore raft

On the way to the railway station someone stole our Flood Relief purse, replaced every single coin with buttons, and put the purse back into Clubfoot's pocket without either of us noticing. When we did notice, we were almost at the railway station.

"Daylight robbery," said Clubfoot, in an attempt to use phrases that were appropriate for the occasion. We could see everyone clumped together on the platform, boxed in by bold and innovative luggage. They all had new suitcases that glowed and sliced through your skin if you touched them the wrong way.

"Ours is coming later," Clubfoot lied. "It's been sent on. It's on the way. It's steel blue. It has flowers on it."

Everyone was happy for our new luggage and said it was smart that we had sent it on. They said wasn't it grand to be going like this and we said yes it was and smiled and shook our hands like the excitement was too much to bear. The first train came and we clambered on, helping people stow luggage and seat themselves. Then we clambered off saying there was no room and we'd catch the next one. When the last train started to leave, people stuck their heads out of the windows and told us to stop clowning around and get on the goddamn train already.

"All we have is buttons. Will they let us on with the buttons?" asked Clubfoot. People shook their heads with sympathy. Some of them said what the fuck but they said it with soft eyes that reminded us of dogs and warm pastries. Someone threw us an apple.

"I hope they don't find out that we lied about the luggage," said Clubfoot. "That's what I'm really worried about. They'd be so violent and upset if they found out we lied about the luggage."

A while ago, we had received a Tamil circular, which took us a month to translate because we didn't want anyone to know that we couldn't read Tamil. When we finally figured out what it said, we had one week to meet the Village Officer, get the circular stamped and attested, and collect our Village Evacuation Packet. The Packet included drinking water stamps, milk tokens, egg tokens, and a brochure on incorporating discipline and patriotism into our daily lives. The Village Officer drank tiny plastic cups of tea and told us of the impending flood. It would have rogue waves that would be sixty storeys high, carrying radioactive sea anemones, bright-red algae and monster cephalopods.

"You must leave as soon as possible," he said. "In fact, you should have already left. It's a shame you are still here."

The last train was our only option, he said, and if we sat on the roof it would be less crowded and the breeze would be like real air conditioning. If we missed the last train, he said he would pray for us, although he felt that prayer didn't really accomplish anything.

We watched the last train disappear into the horizon while the station master folded up his flags and took one last look at the otherwise deserted station.

"Why did you miss the last train?" he asked, pointing at Clubfoot's brace. Everyone did that when they spoke to Clubfoot. It was like they were talking to his leg and the rest of him was purely incidental.

"Why did you?" asked Clubfoot.

"I am taking the last bus," said the station master as he walked away. "I guess you will take that too."

"That's right, see you there!" Clubfoot called after him, even though it was a lie and there was no telling what the station master would do if he found out. We watched him disappear into the horizon much like the last train did, shimmering into a tiny spot and then melting into the atmosphere like he had never been a station master at all, just a part of everything else.

"Well I guess we'll drown now," said Clubfoot. "I guess my brace will get rusty as fuck and give me tetanus and my leg will fall off. I guess you'll have to cut my leg off for me when it gets gangrene. I guess having to cut my leg off will make you die of heartbreak."

"I guess," I said.

In the distance I saw a figure walking towards us. Unlike Clubfoot and I who always walked in uneven lines and often forgot where we were going, this figure walked in a straight line like it was intent on killing something. This was Sully, the Americanadian who ran the local whore-house. Sully was a great guy. Clubfoot and I did not get along with a lot of people but Sully was someone we liked because he was such a great guy. He was wearing cargo shorts and carrying four empty water cans. Soon he was standing in front of us, blocking out a sizable portion of the sky.

"You missed the last train, Sully," I said. "You're going to drown and die just like us."

"I'm not too worried, I've got a raft I'm rigging together," said Sully. "Should make it. I'm not too worried."

Clubfoot told Sully about how he was going to lose his leg to gan-grene and I would have to cut it off and die of heartbreak.

"Tell you what, trade me that brace of yours," said Sully. "Trade me that brace and you can hitch a ride on the raft. If it holds I mean. I'm not too worried though."

"Here," I said, handing him our Flood Relief purse. "You can have our buttons too."

Sully strapped the brace to his back and Clubfoot dragged his leg along, breathing loudly through his mouth. As we walked towards the river, Sully dropped the buttons beside him, leaving a trail of bright blue, yellow and red. There were a few greens and oranges and even a purple one. I bent to pick it up but Sully suddenly turned and said "Don't touch that fucking button! Don't touch it! If you touch it I will cut off your fucking hand!" So I didn't touch it because Sully's a great guy and I didn't want it that much anyway. I don't think I would have given him the money purse if I had known there was a purple button in it though.

At the riverbank, Sully's whores were quietly lined up, their black cotton saris wrapped around their shoulders like they were cold.

"I got the heavier ones on the outside and the young ones in the middle so it should hold fine," said Sully.

He strapped the empty water cans to the arms of four tall women. Then they all walked into the river and one by one, they started floating on their backs, littering the surface of the water like dead fish. Each grabbed another's ankle and wrist until a lattice of bodies had formed on the river.

"It would have been stronger if you had man whores," I said. "Men have lighter bone density or something. They are good for floating."

"The only good whore is a dead whore," said Clubfoot.

Sully told us to lie on our backs, to spread the weight. He also said not to worry about his girls because they were used to everything.

"But don't kick them on purpose," said Sully. "Don't be violent or anything."

Clubfoot's bad leg dragged like a dead branch between a girl with a harelip and one who had the hiccups.

"Whores are just like you and me except they are whores," he said.

I could see his head lolling back and forth on someone's scarred stomach. I was almost face to face with a woman who had light brown eyes and whose mouth was opening and closing, like a fish.

"Hi," I said.

Tiny curls of water arched around her lips, rippling over her cheeks so it looked like she was under a slab of glass. Something drifted into her mouth and never came out again. Overhead, we could see helicopters droning lazily like they had no particular place to go. Thick drifts of cloud began to float down and settle on the surface of the water. Sully said the helicopters were a definite sign that it was all starting.

"Are the helicopters going to save us?" I asked. I could see tiny bundles falling away from them, some opening up in midair, scattering the water with packets of dehydrated vegetables long past their expiry dates and brochures about how the United States was our friend and ally. A can of Spam landed on the girl with the harelip and quiet lines of blood opened up across her forehead. The raft began to teeter.

"You ever have Spam?" asked Sully as he pried the harelipped girl loose—her hair curled into her mouth, got entangled with the hair of other girls, then finally waved gently as she started to sink. "Many Indians haven't eaten Spam before. That's so strange, I mean who hasn't eaten Spam?"

"Indians," said Clubfoot. "And certain Africans. And Chinese people probably."

"So weird," said Sully, chuckling and shaking his head. "I mean it's Spam, for Chrissakes!"

The helicopters slowly diminished into tiny black dots and then disappeared entirely from the sky. Four more whores were hit with Spam tins and pried off of the raft—two of them sank, while one floated away, kicking her feet furiously like she thought she could survive and live a good life somewhere else. One whore clung to the raft and we had to beat her off with Clubfoot's brace.

The discontinued packets of dehydrated vegetables and brochures began to sink. We could see lorries, tiny huts and bicycles in the water below us. Clubfoot wanted to know how much longer the whores were going to last. He did not think whores were into longevity and honourable things like that.

"Whores is whores," said Sully with a shrug. "I'm not too worried."

The water turned a dark colour which I thought was purple and Sully and Clubfoot thought was red. We watched Sully eat some ham sandwiches and drink coffee cola. He gave us each a small rock to keep in our mouths. "Suck on them," he said, "it'll keep the saliva flowing. That's important when you've got no food or drink." Sully gave me the smaller one because it was pale with flecks of pink and blue. It tasted cold and a little salty. After a while it didn't taste like anything.

"You're a good man Sully," said Clubfoot. "Really."

The rock clinked against my teeth and I thought this must be something a child would do on a warm, summer day when it is unhungry and alright. The whores moved gently under me, their chalky, tired faces hanging quietly in the dark water. One of them let go. I watched her beat her arms against the water, then disappear into a pile of dirty clouds.

how to wear
an indian village

Park the car next to a vendor selling tender coconuts. Ask how the crop has been while you weigh each coconut in your hand. Do not smile when you hear the water splashing inside like a secret waterfall. Wear sunglasses.

When they ask where you're from, say you are from Chennai. Say it with a drawl, like it is an American word. Do not say you are from Madras. If you are a man, have two tender coconuts even though they will make you feel thirsty once you get back in the car. If you are a woman, drink half a coconut and give the rest to the man.

Waylay children with bicycles. Grab the handlebars and insist you will only take the cycle down the road and back. Ride with one village child attached to your back and one seated on the handlebars. Make sure someone takes pictures of you. Show your teeth when you smile.

Promise the children that you will send copies of every photograph that was taken. Write their addresses down in English. Make them promise to wait for your letter everyday. Make them say "Yes, we promise" in unison.

Do not stay more than twenty-two minutes. As the car pulls away, wave once and quickly roll up the window.

Two weeks later, you will find abandoned slips of addresses under the car mats. Stuff these into an old cigarette carton and toss it into one of the rabbit-shaped garbage cans in the nearest park.

Keep the pictures.

the ash eaters

We drew maps. We made a Power of Positive Action Map to show how sand from Parangipettai pushed its way towards Chidambaram. We made a Heartless Fuck Map from diagrams of reproductive systems while suicidal ash trickled from our lips. B. Lakshmi said the ash came from cremation grounds and we were going to get massive bad karma anemia. We said *vasadhi mappillai,* dragging out the words like we were going to rape her. Then we made an Anemia Map filled with islands of hard-boiled eggs and rivers of iron tonic. B. Lakshmi drew stick figures drowning in the river and said that was us. A year later her body sat up in her funeral pyre like she had suddenly remembered something. Fat flakes of ash hung in the air while a man beat down her burning chest with a stick.

the tar heroin guide to melting a snowman

1.

When he admits that it was just a line, that it was someone else's line, that he just saw it from a distance sparkling on a mirror like a stripe of salt, ask him if it looked dangerous. Ask him if he got any on his fingers, whether he could smell it from that far away. Ask him if it was risky to be so close to a line of cocaine and if people called it "snow" or "swag". Tell him that you think "snow" is a better word for it and you don't really like the term "booger sugar". Tell him that you've never met anyone who's seen a real line of cocaine before. List out the other things you have not seen in real life, like steak, golf clubs, hash browns, Chanel No. 5, anal beads, pancakes, elderly Latino women, dildos, World War II memorials, Catholic priests, champagne and homosexuals. When he tells you that he ate a steak once or that his friend plays golf, say really? Say this with your eyes wide and your lips parted. Allow your hand to fall on his upper thigh like a dropped handkerchief. Wait.

2.

When he is dragging his tongue down your chest, call him Snowman but don't say this out loud. Visualize lines of cocaine running through him like stripes of salt. Then think of snow, not cocaine but real snow.

Ensure that you remember its key elements like coldness, its tendency to melt and the fact that it ultimately turns into water. Stay focused. Do not think of white flour, sugar, or Colgate tooth powder. Wait until the Snowman is breathing gently in your ear, his body relaxed against you like a crumpled blanket. Then tell him you saw a documentary on tar heroin once. Open this conversation by saying, "hey remember when you saw that line of cocaine?" Tell him that the documentary was not about cocaine and that you always thought tar heroin was made from tar. Admit that you don't really know anything about heroin although you think it's neat that "heroin" and "heroine" both sound the same if you say it in American. Call yourself the Tar Heroin but do not say this out loud either.

3.

Spend weekends at his house by falling asleep in his bed during the nights and forgetting to leave in the mornings. Feed him strong filter coffee decoction with a spoon while you both watch documentaries about drug addicts. Make sure the coffee is very dark and very sweet. When they show open-mouthed teenagers melting tar heroin over distracted flames, put the spoon in your mouth. Feel the coffee slip down your throat and then feel your heart tremble like a dry leaf. Tell yourself that this is what doing drugs is like. Whenever the Snowman starts rubbing his face, take his hands into yours and say "what baby?" Then feed him more coffee with the spoon. Watch him and the documentaries intently. In the beginning, when the coffee is still warm, use phrases like "this is so sad", "drugs are terrible" and "what a waste of life". Later on, use phrases like "that guy is good-looking even though he's a junkie", "heroin isn't as expensive as I thought it would be" and "how come they can talk normally if they are on drugs?" Ask him if the cocaine he saw is like the cocaine in the documentary. When he says he wants to stop watching, say "okay baby, okay." Ask him about his family. Tell him to tell you everything. Say, "I want to know everything about you. Everything. Tell me everything." Keep the documentary on so you can still see the junkies, their spoons and the blood spilling from their clogged veins when he tells you that he doesn't speak to his father anymore.

4.

Go to his house with a bag of bagels. Tell him they were made by real Jewish people. When you hand them to him, accidentally mention how much they cost and then say you are so stupid because you didn't want him to know. While he is eating and his eyes are starting to soften, ask him about his grandmother. Listen to him with your wrists exposed so he can see the crisscross of your veins and the bracelets etched into the base of your palm. Ask him about his school and what he did during the holidays when he was a child. Later, when he has fallen asleep, trace the veins in his neck. Press them gently and feel them bump against your finger like the head of a playful puppy. Picture yourself standing barefoot inside his veins while a slow, sticky stream of black swallows your skin in warm mouthfuls. Think of molasses and melted black licorice. Then think of tar. Write the word "Tar Heroin" on the wall and feel the words bump against your finger as you write. When he wakes up bleary-eyed and dry-mouthed, unsure of what you are doing there, feed him hot water with a spoon. Then kiss him gently, repeatedly, until he falls asleep again.

5.

Make the bed but do not wash his clothes or do the dishes in the sink. Stack the refrigerator with bottles of water. Throw away the milk. Tell him that his cough sounds bad. Keep telling him this until he starts coughing. When he lies down, sit in the other room until he asks you what you're doing over there and if you will come and sit with him. Sit beside him and say, "you are a motherfucking mess, homeboy, a hot, hot, motherfucking mess." Use words you have heard in the documentaries like "smack", "muscling" and "skin-popping" even though you don't really know what they mean. Lie beside him and listen to his uneven, shallow breathing as he falls asleep. Sink the tips of your fingers into his arm and quietly rifle through his tendons like you are looking through a stash of hidden letters. Peer up into his chest cavity and follow the white lines that have clenched over his bones and muscles like frost. Count the stray white flakes that swirl around the base of his throat and fall into your hair and hands. Climb his ribcage and look at his internal organs like you're looking at animals in the zoo. Then lean forward and gently, repeatedly, lick his heart.

6.

Call his mother and tell her that he is not sick but he is not doing too well. Promise to stay with him until she arrives and to leave as soon as she gets here. Prop him up on the bed and watch his head nod forward, then suddenly jerk backward. Nod and jerk your head along with him. When he opens his eyes and tries to focus, cup his face in your hands and say "You picked a fine time to leave me Lucille." Put your forehead against his and say this to him softly, again and again. Let his mouth fall open. Watch the tiny white flakes drift out, landing on the folds of his neck, building gentle waves on his dry chest. Watch them melt, pulling his skin down into every drop that soaks and spreads into the dirty bed sheet. Say "you okay baby?" and run your fingers through his damp hair. Put your head on his chest and listen, first to the uneven murmur of his heart and then to the sound of his fingers dripping to the floor.

the twins

When Anand was fifteen, he threatened to jump off the roof unless the thirteen-year-old girl next door said she loved him. He was standing on the ledge, his gangly arms and legs cutting jagged lines against the sky. The girl was at her window, looking up at him with wide, terrified eyes as beads of sweat gently blossomed on her upper lip. Kavitha was telling her to just say it, because it was just I love you and didn't mean anything. It was when Anand pretended to almost fall off the ledge that I saw the twins—he had chained them to his waist and they were squalling, grasping desperate fistfuls of air with their tiny hands, the skin on their heads already splitting into velvety petals of dark red.

Later that evening, when the thirteen-year-old girl was being blamed and beaten by her uncle for Anand's behaviour, Anand explained that he had just taken the twins with him for good luck. He peered into the box where they both lay shivering, chunks of turmeric sticking to the splits in their skin. One was sleeping but the other was looking up at Anand, its mouth open in a small, mournful "o".

"Hey kicklee kicklee," said Anand, tickling its bloated stomach. "Hey kicklee paya."

"Fuck off," it said, trying to kick Anand in the chin.

"Kicklee paya," said Anand, pressing his finger into its face until it started to beat its little arms against his broad hand. He only stopped when someone from the kitchen said the food was ready—they had made him chicken and fried fish as a reward for not killing himself. Kavitha and I sat with the box between us, watching the twin cough and shudder.

"I'm going to kill myself," it wailed, "I'm going to kill both of us. It's what I'm going to do."

"I know," said Kavitha, stroking its head.

Later that night, our grandfather took the twins and said that if we ever saw Anand go near their box again, we were supposed to tell him so he could break Anand's arms and legs.

•

Over the next four years, Anand threatened six more girls with suicide. The thirteen-year-old girl moved away and a tailor set up shop next door. A tiny tree with pale green leaves grew so resiliently on one of the twin's backs that it seemed like the twin was finally going to die. But the tree eventually withered, falling away in moist, black lumps that smelled like mud. Anand left home, disappearing one night with anything of value he could find in the house.

When I saw him again, our grandfather was dead. Kavitha had left long ago and nobody knew where she was. The house was empty except for me and some broken chairs. Anand arrived with a pot belly and an indifferent five-year-old girl on his arm whom he kept plying with cream biscuits and promises that they would be leaving soon. He sat in the room where he had once tried to suffocate one of the twins—his stomach strained against his shirt and a heavy smell of body odour settled over everything.

"I wanted her to see them," said Anand. "Are they with you?"

"Is she your daughter?" I asked.

"This is Ammu," he said, trying to wipe the girl's nose with a bright blue handkerchief. I watched as he awkwardly grabbed her chin, and then muttered something as she pushed him away.

"So they're with you then," he said. "They must be with you."

The twins had been handed down in our family for generations because we couldn't get rid of them. They were small and speckled with scars from the various times people had tried to kill them. We kept them in a broken wooden box that smelled like cough syrup and was covered in newspaper cuttings of Ian Botham. Nobody knew much about them, except that they looked like small grey stones when they were sleeping. Their skin split when they were upset, their limbs were prone to breaking and seeds sometimes took root in their skin. The only time they had ever been outside was when Anand had taken them to the roof.

"I don't have them," I said.

"I just wanted her to see them," said Anand. "Maybe take a picture. I have a camera on my phone."

"They aren't here," I said. "I don't have them."

"That's fine," he said. "I just wanted to show her, that's all."

He asked how I was doing and said I should visit him sometime because it wasn't that far, one straight bus. Then he asked for a glass of water. I went to the kitchen and waited by the stove. I could hear him yanking open different almirahs, shuffling through old clothes and papers. Then I heard him say "ah!"

From the window I watched him, almost running, the girl under one arm, the wooden box under the other. He hadn't even bothered to remove the old saris it was wrapped in and they trailed behind him, sometimes snapping at his heels, sometimes curling into the late afternoon sunshine like they were waving goodbye.

•

The new box was smaller but cleaner and only smelled like cardboard. The sleeping twin was curled around a rubber ball that I had given them to play with. The other was looking up at me—the plant that had taken root behind its ear was already dying, its leaves curling up like small fists.

"I'm going to kill myself," it said softly.

I pinched off some of the dead leaves. They came away easily, falling gently into the palm of my hand.

"I'm going to kill both of us," said the twin. "It's what I'm going to do."

"I know," I said.

I touched its forehead, tracing a scar that ran down to its neck and then disappeared somewhere inside its wrinkled skin.

I should have fucked with my eyes closed.

I should have danced to Barbie Girl.

I should have left by now.

the decline and fall of western dance in a south indian women's college

In the middle of the second verse, the girl beside me stopped dancing. Her body suddenly relaxed and rivulets of sweat trickled down her forehead in twisted sparkles. She seemed to hang there, inches above the floor. Then she turned and walked off the stage, leaving a trail of dusty, indifferent glitter. It was as if she had evaporated and that was all that was left of her.

"Where's she going?" said the girl behind me.

I shrugged.

"I'm going to see," said the girl. "I'm going to see where she went."

She walked off the stage, trailed by another girl who seemed to follow her as an afterthought. At some point the music stopped and the few of us who were still dancing came to uncertain standstills, afraid something was happening that we didn't know about. The GumChewer kept dancing in the front row, her lips distractedly mouthing the words. We watched her, hands on our hips, sweat spangling our faces.

"Girls! You're requested to leave the stage, girls," said the thin, sad voice of the PT Ma'am. The GumChewer kept moving and we kept watching her, periodically brushing sweat from our arms and faces.

"Stop dancing," said the PT Ma'am, more thinly and sadly than before. "You are requested to please stop dancing. The girl who is still dancing is requested to stop dancing as soon as possible. Immediately."

Someone hissed at me from the wings.

"Take your friend off!"

"She's not my friend," I said, watching The GumChewer dance like she didn't care about anything.

"Just take her off. You have to leave the stage!"

"Why?"

"You've been disqualified! You have to go!"

"Go where? Hey, how come you guys stopped the music?"

A huddle of girls wearing badges that said Discipline Committee shuffled onto the stage and stood there, unwilling to do anything. The mic gave a staticy whine and the PT Ma'am's voice wailed like a heartbreak: "The Discipline Committee members are kindly requested to escort the girls off stage. Thank you. Immediately."

We stumbled through the sudden darkness towards the exit, the Discipline Committee members hovering around us, hissing instructions to each other in Tamil. I wanted to hiss in Tamil too, to show them that I was just like them even though I didn't have a Discipline Committee badge. I reached out and touched the hair of a Discipline Committee girl who was walking next to me. It was surprisingly soft and left a slick of oil on my fingers. When we got outside, I turned to smile at her but she, along with the rest of the Discipline Committee girls, was already gone. Those of us who were still left from the Western Dance Group began to fray and float off in groups of three and four. Soon everyone had left except me and The GumChewer. She was still swaying back and forth, humming softly to herself.

"I think we got disqualified," I said.

"You mean like the whole college?" she said, swaying.

"No, us. The Western Dance Group."

"Chee."

"I'm serious. I think it just happened. Like, just now."

"What the fuck? Why? How can they disqualify us?"

The GumChewer clicked her tongue, her attention distracted by the piles of popcorn that had collected on the sides of the walkway. I followed her gaze and suddenly wondered what she looked like when she was at home. I wondered what she watched on television, what she ate, what her mother looked like. I wondered if she ever wondered about me in that way. I thought that she probably didn't and this was both a relief and sad.

•

During my first year, a senior named Saraswathi who everyone called Saras would stand in front of us during dance practice and stare at me like she wanted to kill me. She was severe and straight as a tightly-folded umbrella, her eyes a pair of salty black dots. Once Saras had stared at The GumChewer like that and The GumChewer had fainted. After that, Saras made it a point to refer to her as my fainting friend, even though I told her she wasn't my friend, that I didn't even know her real name.

"Everyone in this group is your friend," Saras had said, "You understand? Understand what I'm saying?"

I had nodded even though I had no idea what she was talking about.

When Saras wasn't staring at me, she would look over my shoulder and say "disappointing, girls" or "not happening, just not happening". Then she would shake her head in a very slow and deliberate way and the other seniors would agree with her in hushed tones.

During her final year, Saras got a part in a Tamil movie as "the girl from America", who kept getting slapped by the hero. She dyed her hair black, which none of us could understand because her hair used to be black anyway and now it looked navy blue though no one had the guts to tell her this. Saras would burst into practice with three or four girls and stand with her hands on her hips, one corner of her upper lip hooked up into a soft snarl. She called us cuntsuckers while snapping foreign bubble gum that smelled minty and expensive. "You're a bunch of motherfucking cuntsuckers, you know that? Fuckall cuntsuckers. That's what you all are."

She would spit these words out as if they were small, jagged pits, her chin jutting out like she was ready to fight us all at once. She did this when we danced, when we sat on the ground panting during the break, when we left practice. Once a girl we had all referred to as Madurai Chikki asked her why she kept saying that to us, what was the need to keep saying such words? The next week Madurai Chikki was cut from the squad and if we saw her on campus and called out to her, she would not look at us.

At the end of her final year, Saras organized five attendancecompulsory farewell parties for the Western Dance Group. They were held at the canteen, at the practice area, at a restaurant I couldn't afford, at someone's house and at a coffee shop none of us could find because it was actually a table and some chairs on the roof of someone's building, which made us all feel cheated. The concept of the farewell party coupled with Saras' enthusiasm for saying goodbye and being heartbroken weighed us all down like a fist grinding into our collective heart. For the first few farewell parties, we hugged and cried, our hands clutching so desperately at each others' shirts that they left crumpled mountains in their wake. After all, we had walked to places together, waited together; our shoulders, hands and hair had touched in familiar ways as we argued, laughed and made fun of people together. We knew how the contours of each other's bodies looked against damp t-shirts, we knew what each girl's sweat smelled like, what she liked to drink when we went to the canteen, what she looked like when she was panting. It seemed impossible to know each girl in this way and simply walk away from it, to picture a life beyond this, beyond each other. But by the third farewell party, we forgot to feel these things, or we felt them at the wrong time, for the wrong reasons. The GumChewer suddenly started to miss Madurai Chikki and I, for the first time ever, became homesick.

And then the year ended, abruptly and unexpectedly, and everyone disappeared. Overnight, the canteen became bereft of food, offering only a few bars of white chocolate and warm 7-Up. Lecturers walked in late, wearing salwars and holding fat, pouty children. The farewell parties ended and the intense, painful feeling of loss and heartbreak dissipated into the emptiness of the deserted campus. Everyone slowly became unreachable by phone or went out of town, without saying where they were going or when they expected to be back.

"They'll be back for my wedding," said Saras confidently. She had swiftly put the farewell parties down and picked up her wedding like it was the next thing to be passed around. I did not know who Saras was marrying but I was almost tempted to go, simply to see what he looked like. But I didn't. Nobody did. While we were all busy being someplace else and doing other things, Saras was successfully married off and sent to live in America. She, along with the farewell parties and the rest of that year, ended neatly, like the snipping of a piece of string.

I did not think of her at all until a few months into my final year when she started sending me letters. They came in thick white envelopes and were filled with curled, blue writing that was sometimes scratched out, sometimes crossed over. She called me Junior. The beginning of each letter went into extensive detail about things she had bought, people she had seen, "Indian" people she had eaten meals with. The rest of her letters were filled with questions about the Western Dance Group. She wanted to know what was going on, what competitions we were going for, what songs we had chosen. Tell me everything, she would say. I want to know everything.

In the beginning, I would take these letters to practice because I did not know what else to do with them. Everyone passed them around, read them and said that Saras had been so great, the group just wasn't the same without her and we all missed her so much. By the time her fourth letter came, the girls wanted to know why she didn't have better things to do in America than write stupid letters to people who didn't give a flying fuck about her. They wanted to know why she had called us cuntsuckers. Why did she dye her hair black that one time? Did she know that it looked fucking blue? At some point, I suggested that we all write her back and The GumChewer had slapped me on the arm—"*You* write her back. She wrote to *you*. Write and ask her about the cuntsucker thing. That's something we all want to know. No, you guys? And ask her if she knew that her hair was fucking blue that one time."

In a desperate attempt to make Saras' letters stop, I wrote to her in large, illegible handwriting. I went into unnecessary detail about the construction work in the outdoor auditorium. I lied and said we were being stalked by a photographer from *Kumudham* who was trying to take pictures of us while we changed. I told her we were in talks to do an item number for a Tamil movie and the group was split on whether we should do it or not. One letter was filled with promises to send pictures that had never been taken although I could see them very clearly in my mind, and was sure they would be fabulous pictures if they could only exist.

Saras kept writing back. When I returned from quarterly or half-yearly holidays, there would be letters from her waiting for me in the small hostel mailbox, lying awkwardly among the smaller, thinner local letters. The hostel people started calling her my American boyfriend. She's not even my friend, I would say. Then why does she keep writing to you, they asked. I never had an answer to this.

•

I spent every Sunday with Bose. I had done this for the past three years, leaving the hostel early in the morning and weaving through streets that were sometimes dotted with grimy puddles, sometimes misted over with violent, disoriented clouds of dust. When I reached his house, I had a hot water bath and washed my hair with his shampoo. When I was done, I smelled his soap, his shaving lotion, and his deodorant; I refolded his towel, placing it neatly on the rod he had "organized" under the window. It was really just a length of plastic pipe that he had hung from the rusty window bars. But it was his towel rack and he had organized it.

While I was doing this, Bose would go out and come back with his fingers twisted and weighed down with plastic bags filled with cheap, greasy food, his mouth pulled up in an excited smile. He arranged everything on the single table he had in his room, showing me the boxes and bags of the things he had bought without opening them, without letting me touch them. I never understood why he did this because he never let me take anything from the table. Even if he was half-asleep, he would get up and get me what I wanted, laying it out on one of his two plastic plates, with one of his plastic spoons and a single napkin saved from his sporadic restaurant visits.

We would spend the day sitting on a straw mat, watching movies about vampires or cops who were out for revenge. If the electricity went for a very long time and we couldn't think of anything to talk about, we would lie there, part of me listening to the sounds of his breathing or the feel of his mouth gently moving along my skin. The other part of me would trace the cracks on the wall, the light streaming in from the window, the lines of his shoulders and back.

We always ended up tangled in each other, arms propped onto legs, heads on shoulders, fingers lost around torsos or in each other's hair. In the evening, we would blearily look at how we had twisted ourselves into each other, the heavy heat of the afternoon still clinging to our faces. "Hey! How'd all this happen?" Bose would ask brightly, again and again until I finally cracked a sleepy, sweat-stained smile.

He was the only person who asked about Saras. When he was changing movie CDs or washing one of the plastic spoons, he would suddenly ask, "So what's Saras saying?" Because of this, I kept trying to leave her letters in his house. Every so often, I would bring them wrapped in an old plastic bag and leave them on a chair or under a table. But before I left, he would always hand them to me and say "You forgot this." Once I had tried to explain that I needed to leave them here because I didn't have enough room at the hostel. "What made you think there was room here?" he asked, looking at his cramped room, the TV on the floor, his mattress rolled into the corner and carefully covered with a cotton cloth. "Just keep it anywhere," I had said. "It doesn't matter if they get lost." But he would shake his head and say they were letters, like that meant something special.

In the evenings, Bose and I walked up and down the crowded street outside his house to work off the weight of the movies and the afternoon heat. He said this was important because we hadn't had any exercise all day. Sunday was the only day he didn't do his evening run; otherwise he never missed a day, even if he was sick, even if it was raining and the roads were flooded.

"I hope you're not missing your run because of me," I said to him once. "I mean, I can just hang out here and wait for you."

"No no," he had said briskly. "Let's walk. Sundays are for walking."

Sometimes the heat would hit us like a thick, dirty blanket. But we kept walking, moving together with each step and swerve like we were one body. Sometimes the sun would set into a gauzy film of purple dust and I would hear children laughing. Other times I would step in spit or see a pair of chicken feet lying in the gutter. The GumChewer saw us once and said we looked androgynous. Another time she said we looked like brothersister. She started calling Bose the brothersister fellow, possibly because she didn't really know what androgynous meant.

•

The day after being disqualified, the Western Dance Group was summoned to a classroom that I had never noticed before. It was behind the auditorium and had a tiny brown door that looked like it should lead into a secret garden. I wondered how many other rooms there were like this, rooms I never knew existed but appeared behind innocuous brown doors. The room had seven chairs and a patch of black painted on the wall, on which someone had written *bless our sweet classroom* in pink chalk.

Very suddenly a lecturer appeared, bustling in like she was carrying bad news that she wanted to get rid of as soon as possible. This same lecturer had once told us we were so talented and precious for the college. She had said this to all of us but she had stood beside me, her arm around my waist like she specifically meant I was the talented and precious one. Now she did not notice me at all. She stood there, arms folded. Then she said she wanted to know if we thought we were very smart. She said she had never seen such a shameful display by *any* group of girls before, much less from this college, much less from such a prestigious group like the Western Dance Group. Then she shook her head and said she just didn't know. If this was what we thought was okay to do, if this is what we were prepared to do to ourselves and our college, then she just didn't know. I wanted to stand up and shout *Don't give up on us, Ma'am! Don't give up on me! Please don't give up on me! You said I was precious!*

"What's going on?" The GumChewer whispered to me. "What is she saying?"

"I think she's yelling at us," I said.

"Why?"

"We got disqualified, no?"

"You mean the college?"

"No, us. Western Dance Group."

"When?"

"Yesterday."

"When did this happen?"

"When we were dancing, we got disqualified. Remember?"

The GumChewer frowned. Then she shook her head.

"I don't remember that at all," she said slowly.

"How can you not remember that!" I snapped, grabbing her hand. "You were there! You were dancing on stage! How can you not remember? Why do you keep saying you can't remember when you were there?"

I suddenly realized that the lecturer had stopped talking and everyone was looking at me. The GumChewer slowly pulled her hand out of my grasp, pursing her lips and frowning. I wanted to hold her face in my hands and make her look at me and say *You were there. I was there. Think. Try and remember. We were both there. I know you'd remember if you just tried.*

The GumChewer started shaking her head. "Really don't remember any of this," she said. "At all."

•

The Western Dance Group was formally disbanded and kept under indefinite suspension, which meant we all had to go back to class. Some girls went back to departments like History and Mathematics, which made the rest of us gasp in surprise and say things like "She doesn't *look* like she's in History, no?" Some girls went directly back to their assigned seats, pulled out textbooks and took notes like they had always been there. Other girls did not come to college at all—without Western Dance, it seemed impossible for them to exist and they dissolved into thin air, their names appearing in the corners of department blackboards under headings like "attendance case". Still others dragged themselves around, utterly isolated and alone like new girls in class. They helplessly peered at textbooks that had never been cracked open and faced the reality of months of material that had to be read and understood in a few weeks.

I brought one borrowed blue pen and a piece of paper to class each day. I pretended to take notes but I was really writing things like

Nobody. Not even the Rain has such small boobies.
Have patience with everything unresolved in your heart.
Have patience. Everything is unresolved in your heart.
Everybody grab a body pump it like you want somebody.

Some lecturers saw me and said things like "nice to see you taking an interest in your studies as well as extracurricular activities." Others smirked at me and said "so no more dancing for you, ah? You know what class this is? What department?"

When The GumChewer was part of the Western Dance Group, she walked slowly, swaying slightly, carrying nothing but her bike keys. But once the Western Dance Group was dissolved, she became someone who was always walking quickly, looking at her watch, weighed down with books. She sat in the front row of her class like a tightly coiled spring, answering questions, discussing things with lecturers. Whenever I saw her, she was either framed by classroom windows or she was a figure in the distance walking to her bike. Once we ran into each other outside the canteen and she hugged me like she could not believe I was still there, that I still existed.

"What machan?" she said, smiling and shaking her head. I looked at the books tucked neatly into her arms.

"You're Eco?" I said with surprise.

"Didn't you know?"

"No, I thought you were Corporate," I said. "Or B.Com or something."

"Chee! Do I look like B.Com to you?"

She talked about upcoming tests, her recent visits to the library, about a project that a lecturer was trying to get her involved in.

"And you?" she said. "What have you been up to? How's your boyfriend?"

"What boyfriend?"

"That guy I saw you with, that brothersister fellow."

"He's not my boyfriend."

"I thought he was your boyfriend. Don't you hang out at his house?"

"That doesn't make him my boyfriend."

She nodded and looked down at the books in her arms, counting them under her breath. She said we should meet up soon and then she was gone. In the distance, a girl was calling to her and pulling out a large book from a plastic bag. The GumChewer walked towards her, like she had never danced in her life.

It was at that moment that I realized I still didn't know what The GumChewer's real name was. It had never occurred to me to ask. For some reason, it did not seem like an important thing to know.

•

That week, I got two letters from Saras. The first one said she was coming to see us, all of us. She wanted to see what we had been working on. She wanted to meet up for a big lunch. She wanted us all to come home, since none of us had managed to come for the wedding. She wanted to go dancing one night. She definitely wanted to go dancing, just the girls, husbands not allowed. She wrote this in large letters, underlining it three times. The second letter gave me a breakdown of her plans. All of them involved coming to the hostel first and picking me up. Be ready, she wrote. Be ready to have some fun. Be ready to go out. Be ready to do some real dancing when I get there.

I hid these two letters under my roommate's mattress. I then decided it would be a good idea to hide all the letters this way, slipping a couple under one mattress, maybe distribute them evenly among all the rooms. I wondered why this hadn't occurred to me before. Instead of trying to keep them in Bose's house, I could have just slid them under someone's bedding, drowned them in the college "lily pond", set them on fire on the roof of the Economics building on a Sunday evening when the campus was completely empty. There were suddenly so many possibilities I hadn't even considered, so many things I could do. But that night, my roommate handed back the two letters—she had stapled them shut to prove she hadn't read them.

A few nights later, Saras called the hostel, just as I was going for dinner.

"Hey Junior," she said, "What the fuck you doing?"

"What?" I said.

"I said what the fuck you doing?"

"Who is this?"

"Hey," she said suddenly sounding wrinkled and unsure. "It's me, da."

I waited to see if she would say her name but she didn't.

"Oh," I said. "Hey."

"You know who this is, right?"

"Yeah. Hi."

"So you forget your seniors so quickly, ah? Can't write me back also?"

"I have to go for dinner. They'll be closing the mess soon."

"How soon?"

"In an hour."

"Ample time. You can talk to me."

"Okay."

"So I'm coming down Tuesday, okay? We'll see the girls, I want to see what ya'll have been working on. Then I'm taking you out, I want to have some nice decent food. Then need to get some stuff stitched also. Then you come home for a while, you can tell me everything I've missed. And show me all those pics you kept promising to send but never did. And I've got some stuff for you. Nothing fancy, just stuff I wanted to send but couldn't. You know."

"Right," I said. I thought that she had probably brought me candy or deodorant. People always came back from America with candy and deodorant.

"It's okay," she said.

"What's okay?"

"The pics. I know it's hard to send and stuff and I know you must have been busy." Her voice sounded unexpectedly soft and sad. I suddenly wanted to hear her say cuntsucker. I wanted to hear her spit it out from the back of her throat, like she was ready to fight everyone, like she wanted to kill me.

"Okay Junior," she said suddenly. "You go eat."

"Okay."

"Tuesday, okay? You be ready."

"Cuntsucker," I whispered, very gently.

"What?"

"Nothing. I'll see you."

•

That Sunday, Bose and I watched westerns because he thought it would be a nice change from the vampire and cop movies. I had taken every single letter Saras had written me, taped them all together, covered them in paper, wrapped them in two thick plastic bags and taped the plastic bags shut. The bundle of letters now looked like the parcels of drugs I had seen gangsters hand to each other in some movie. I kept them behind us, while I eyed the corners of Bose's house, trying to find the right hiding place. I found two statistics textbooks, well-thumbed, the pages slightly yellowed and studded with notes made with an eager and determined hand. If this was Bose's handwriting, it was the first time I was seeing it and I didn't know what to make of it—it seemed uncomfortably feminine and loud. I quickly shut the books and stacked them in front of the bundle of letters. A little later, I pulled my top off and draped it casually over the books.

Somewhere during the second movie, the electricity went off. We stared at the black screen for a few seconds, as if the movie was still running.

"Our Western Dance Group got suspended," I said. "We're not allowed to dance anymore."

"Wow," said Bose. He seemed genuinely surprised by this. I looked at his dark head, the hair plastered down at the nape of his neck. "Wow," he said again.

"Yeah."

"What did you guys do?"

"I don't really know," I said. I remembered the girl walking off the stage, The GumChewer's dancing and how she couldn't understand what we had done. I guess I couldn't understand either.

"You guys like, knife a judge? Or something?" said Bose. I stared at him for a few seconds. Speckles of sweat had blossomed on the bridge of his nose.

"I'm kidding," he said. "But…what did you do? Must have been pretty bad, right? I mean to get suspended and shit. Right? I mean-"

I kept looking at him and he suddenly smiled in a way that made his mouth look like a fish caught in a shallow pool of water.

"Saras called me," I said.

"Hey," he said loudly, breaking into a grin and slapping my knee. "That's nice! What's the occasion? How is she?"

"She's coming down," I said, looking at his large, gentle hand. "Or she's already here. She's coming down or already here, one of the two."

"So you'll be able to meet her!"

The beads of sweat on his nose were slowly pulling together. It was like they were holding hands and then pulling each other into themselves.

"Well," said Bose. "It will be nice for you to see her."

I nodded and slowly ran my finger down the bridge of his nose, feeling the sweat smear warmly and slickly into my skin. Bose leaned his forehead against mine and sighed, like he was very tired and wanted to go home. I turned and saw our reflection in the black TV screen. We looked strikingly clear and bright, like a jewellery ad. Then the TV flickered on and we disappeared under bad Native Americans and Mexicans with guns.

•

On Monday morning, every single tap in the college hostel dried up. The girls sat at the side entrance and the hostel warden walked back and forth in her nightdress. Once she stopped and pointed at us with her middle finger.

"See ma? This is why you need to have valid local guardian! No water means where will you go? Where will I go?"

When the water came, we were rationed one bucket per person. Everyone was instructed to go home or to their local guardian's house. Anyone caught washing their hair or clothes would be severely fined. Anyone suffering from diarrhoea was asked to meet the hostel warden separately. By afternoon, the only girls left in the hostel were three girls from Nagaland and me. We sat by the telephone like we were waiting for someone to call us and tell us what was going to happen next.

"You're in Western Dance, no?" said one of the Nagaland girls. "That's cool. I used to play guitar."

"I have a friend who used to play guitar in church," said another girl.

"That's cool," I said and the Nagaland girls nodded. In the evening, The GumChewer came to see me. She looked radiant and unfamiliar—it was the same look I had seen on the faces of girls in the hostel who had spent a good day studying and were filled with meaty and wholesome learning.

"There's no water," I said.

"No water where?" said The GumChewer.

"Here. In the hostel."

"Why?"

"I don't know. I only got one bucket of water today. Everyone's gone, only me and the Nagaland girls are left."

"Nagaland? You have girls from Nagaland here?"

"Sure. Why?"

"Wow. That's far away, no?"

I nodded.

•

That night, two of the Nagaland girls left. The remaining Nagaland girl was leaving in the morning to stay with the cousin of the friend who used to play guitar in church. The warden called me down to her room and said I looked very pale and should start taking an iron tonic. Then she said I had to leave by tomorrow afternoon.

"Don't you have friends in the Western Dance Group?" she said. "Where do you go on Sundays? Why can't you stay there?"

"Yes ma'am," I said and the warden told me to take iron tablets because some iron tonics had mercury in them.

That night we were given unlimited curd and applams with dinner. The warden let us watch TV with her. At night, I stared at the empty cots in my room, watching the reflections of the sodium lamps outside slide across them. I could hear the phone ringing downstairs, the sound of the watchman whacking the tree trunks as he walked passed them. During my first year, I had always been too excited to sleep. My mind would keep making lists of things I was going to do and try and be. The next day I would fall asleep in class and dream that everyone smelled like an old wooden desk and loved me so much it made their noses bleed.

I should have smiled more, I thought to myself. *Especially when Saras used to get in my face and call me a cuntsucker. I should have smiled. I should have showed her my teeth.*

I should have smoked more.

I should have fucked with my eyes closed.

I should have danced to Barbie Girl.

I should have left by now.

The phone stopped ringing and for a moment, the hostel seemed like the quietest, emptiest place on earth.

•

The next morning, I had my last cup of hostel coffee, threw all my belongings into assorted plastic bags and said goodbye to the warden. She told me to study hard and that she hoped I would get married soon. Then she pressed a piece of paper into my hand with the name of an effective, mercury-free iron supplement on it.

"You must take care of your health," she said. "Western Dance means especially. You need to pay attention to all this kind of thing."

On the way out, I saw the Nagaland girl waiting near the college gate and for some reason, I sat down and waited beside her.

"You don't have to," she said. "You don't even know my name, do you?"

I shook my head, suddenly remembering The GumChewer, Madurai Chikki, wondering where they were, what they were doing.

"It's okay," she said. "I don't know your name either."

A little while later, I was on a bus, watching the city collapse awkwardly past my broken window. I thought of how in America, Western Dance was probably not called Western Dance. It was probably just called dance or maybe it was the same as being a cheerleader. I wasn't sure if they had women's colleges or hostels there but if they did, they probably didn't have water problems. And if I was leaving like I was now, I would probably be leaving for Spring Break or to meet my boyfriend's family or to go skiing. I probably wouldn't be on a bus because I would have a second-hand car. Or maybe I would hitchhike and a man with a red baseball cap driving a big rig would pick me up and sell me for a really high price to a brothel in Mexico.

I thought of Saras, waiting for me. It was only later that I remembered Bose would be waiting for me too.

this is us and
this is us outside

The Pepsi Girl will puke all over the table in fourteen minutes. We will watch her and wonder who she is and why she is puking at our table. The Gay Man will start covering the puke with paper napkins. He will not scream "Oh my goodness!" or flutter his hands. We will be stunned by this when we think about it later. We will decide that he probably isn't gay.

The Girl With Razor Blades will find everything incredible and funny, especially the puking Pepsi Girl, the napkins and The Gay Man. She will say, "Look at the fucking pouf, no? Look what he's doing, no? Look at this vomit case, no?" A few days later, when we are talking about the new Rupee symbol and wondering how to draw it, The Girl With Razor Blades will suddenly show us her breasts. She will stand there with her shirt open and we will not know what to do. It will be The Paracetamol Girl who finally says "What the fuck?" The Girl With Razor Blades will say her Malayali grandmother never wore a blouse at all. "Boobs are not a big deal. Don't be so hung up on boobs," she will say and The Paracetamol Girl will say "I don't give a fuck about your Malayali grandmother." Later, we will discover that The Paracetamol Girl used meth on her last trip to the US. We will ask her what it tasted like and if it hurt. She will say she hates the States, she keeps thinking about college and she misses college so much. She will never say she misses us. One month later, she will go to America and never come back and we will never see her again.

I will see The Gay Man once more but I won't tell anyone about it. He will say "What happened to your friend?" and I won't know what he's talking about. "The one that vomited that night," he will say and I will think how after a certain age, one should stop saying "puke" and start saying "vomit". I will imagine The Pepsi Girl's unconscious body being passed around a backroom where she is gang-raped by auto drivers, sons of politicians and hotel staff. "I'm sure she's fine," I will say to The Gay Man. I will not tell him that he is the first gay person I have ever met and that I will never forget him.

We will learn about The Pepsi Girl's alcohol poisoning much later. The Paracetamol Girl will already be gone and we will miss her fiercely when we hear the words "alcohol poisoning". We will all feel responsible. I will ask if the alcohol poisoning means she was gang-raped and everyone will tell me to shut up because the word "rape" will make everyone uncomfortable. The Girl With Razor Blades will call someone to find out what happened but this someone will not remember The Girl With Razor Blades or The Pepsi Girl and they will not know what we're talking about.

At first, we will decide that she did not die. We will tell ourselves that she probably went to work the next day with a hangover and went to the gym in the evening. We will decide that her nickname is Capacity. This will not explain why we called her The Pepsi Girl but we will not discuss that.

Then we will decide that she did die. It was probably her first time drinking. She was probably twenty-two with a younger brother in twelfth standard. Her parents will be more bewildered than sad at her death. They will say "But she studied so well," and they will not understand how a girl who studies so well can become a woman who dies of alcohol poisoning. We will feel sorry for them but we will also think they are stupid. We will be glad they are not our parents.

But we're not thinking of any of that right now. Right now, I'm looking at The Gay Man and wondering if kissing him would be like kissing a girl. The Paracetamol Girl is eating all the food on the table and saying "Everything tastes like shit. I can't believe we're spending money here so we can sit and eat shit." "I know," says The Girl with Razor Blades. "And white women are such fucking whores." She says this loudly, so that the white woman at the next table turns and looks at us.

We will only notice The Pepsi Girl fourteen minutes later, when she pukes all over the table.

everyone does integral calculus

After we looked at the sea, Durai and I turned and looked at the highway. He said the sea would blind us if we stared at it too long. The highway would just make us sad or put us to sleep. We looked at the roadkill and decided to take stock of ourselves.

"Let's retrace the journey, right from the beginning," said Durai. "What did we do to get here?"

Durai went first. He said that when he was a boy he sang devotional songs and his eyes would close of their own accord when he sang the word "God".

"Sing something now," I said. "Anything."

"No."

"Oh, come on. It doesn't have to be about God. Something small. One line."

He rubbed his face and looked over his shoulder at the sea. Then he sang softly in Tamil. *"You're just a doll, I'm just a doll, when you think about it, we're all just dolls."*

I noticed strings of nits shining like beads in his hair.

"Well?" he said.

"You couldn't think of anything else to sing?" I said.

•

I wanted to know why Durai didn't sing anymore.

"Something must have happened," I said. "Someone must have abused you musically."

"Okay, your turn. What did you do to get here?"

"Nothing."

"Think. You must have done something."

"Integral calculus."

"That doesn't count. Everyone does integral calculus."

"Not everyone. Not poor people."

"Even poor people. If they go to school, they do integral calculus."

I thought of picking a louse from his hair when he wasn't looking. I thought of how it would squirm in the centre of my palm like a tiny misshapen star.

•

Durai said we were not getting anywhere so he suggested secrets.

"Okay, go," I said.

"I got thrown in jail when I was in college."

"So?"

"What so? It was jail. Like jail-jail, with bars and shit."

"All guys get thrown in jail when they're in college. They also become drug addicts and fall in love with prostitutes."

"You forgot the motorcycles. We all had motorcycles."

"When I was little I really wanted to be a boy. I wanted to have a name like Sathya and wear hats and sunglasses."

Durai scratched the inside of his wrist like he was trying to open a vein.

"Do you still wish you were a boy?" he asked.

"No. Once my breasts kicked in I changed my mind."

"That's good. I like your breasts."

"I know you do."

•

We were still facing the road but our heads had turned and we were looking at the sea again. We discovered that we had both stolen mercury from our school chemistry labs. Durai had slipped his into his pocket. I had hidden mine in my geometry box. We both had rolled it across our hands and face. I was sure we would get cancer because of this but Durai said it would just make us go crazy. I leaned back and thought about the lice sucking and fucking on his head.

"My neck hurts. Why can't we just face the sea?" I said.

"It's too soon."

"What's that song? About coming too soon or too early? Tickticktick something something?"

"No idea," said Durai.

"Are you sure? I thought everyone knew that song."

I yawned and watched a thick, black louse clamber up through his hair and wave desperately at the sky.

jugni

Jugni always carried herself with an obnoxiously straight spinal column. She didn't know how to slouch and we assumed this was due to a privileged upbringing. News of this assumption and our audacity to have such an assumption sparked off Jugni's first recorded tantrum, where she pulled out a chunk of Azhagu's hair.

Ladies, slouching has nothing to do with privilege and everything to do with bone structure. It has to do with calcium intake and an awareness of one's posture. You may say that these are all signs of privilege. I say you're full of crack. I say you're the stupidest bunch of twat-faced bitches I ever saw.

Azhagu felt that *we* should have taken charge of Jugni's slouch. We should have curled her back for the sake of experiment and experience. After all, it was part of our Womanifesto or Bill of Rights. Once upon a time, a girl had referred to this as The Bill of Tights and Jugni had said that if she ever heard anyone say that again, she would rip their tits off. Because we were all very fond of our tits, we made it a point to call it the Womanifesto, especially when we were around Jugni.

Azhagu resented Jugni's spinal column because her own spine curved so completely it made the back of her neck disappear. We pointed out that all our backs did that. We had even written a collective poem about it.

Look at us.
We think we're vampires or vicious cat-like creatures.
But really,
We're a bunch of turtles trying to get a better look at the sky
And failing.

Our backs made us suffer from malnourishment and a reduced sense of self-worth. The only one who didn't suffer from anything was Jugni.

"It's incorrigible," Azhagu sputtered. "It's the most arrogant spinal column in the world!"

"Not arrogant," I said. "It's... independent."

"Same thing."

"You're just harbouring resentment about that whole hair-pulling thing. And Jugni says that women should never have harbours."

"God, how I hate her. How I hate her spinal column."

Jugni was also the only one who people were thoughtful enough to label. We kept a careful record of what had been said so far:

Jugni is
1. Spirited and sexy like an old acid burn
2. A firefly cut with heroin
3. A bottle of sunshine and soda water
4. Cuddly like an armful of asbestos
5. A tall drink of ice-cold vinegar on a hot day

Somebody had also said that Jugni put the "ho" in "whore" but after extensive discussion and debate, we decided not to put that on the list.

•

For the past few days, reports had trickled in stating that Jugni had killed herself or was murdered or was hibernating, depending on who you asked. The bottom line was that nobody could find her. Azhagu and I took it upon ourselves to investigate. We promised to record everything. They even gave us an expensive camera so that we could take pictures. "Anything that moves you. Think of what Jugni would have done if she had a camera," they said. When we were switching buses in a semi-deserted bus stand, Azhagu traded the camera for two packs of tapioca chips.

"That's it?" I said, staring at the greasy packets in her hand.

"These are garlic tapioca chips, they're very rare. Totally worth it, trust me."

The directions regarding Jugni's whereabouts had been meticulously collected for us on a single sheet of "goodforeign" paper. This was used to wipe Azhagu's hands after she ate both packs of chips.

"Here," she said, handing me the crumpled sheet.

"I'm not touching that."

"It's the directionsinstructions, you have to touch it."

"I am not touching that."

"Fine. Neither am I," said Azhagu and she tossed it into a dry riverbed. The weight of this action hit us later, when we realized that we had no idea where to go.

"You shouldn't have done that," I said.

"I had no choice! You refused to touch it, remember?"

After wandering around for a while, we came to a well. At the bottom was a glistening, crumpled heap of woman with a small metal bucket sitting on top of her. It was an ordinary well, which both of us found very disappointing. The inside was lined with black lichen and tiny powder-blue crabs.

"Look at that," said Azhagu. "We didn't need the instructiondirections after all."

"Jugni *did* advocate water suicide for young women. I even bought the illustrated tutorial. She signed it and everything."

"I knew she was dead. I so knew it."

"I thought she might be rejuvenating herself or something."

"You didn't know her like I did."

I looked around the outside to see if she had scrawled a line of poetry or an expletive before jumping in. But there was nothing.

"I jumped into my first well when I was twelve," said Azhagu. "I just jumped in, no thinking, no warning, nothing, just jumped. And nobody even noticed I was gone. And I got pneumonia."

"You got pneumonia."

"Yes and because of the pneumonia, all my hair fell out and never grew back and this is why I could never get married."

I watched a crab scuttle over the tangles of Jugni's hair. Her hair had never been one of her assets but in death, it seemed very rich, black and worth living for. I had a feeling this was one of the reasons she advocated water suicide. At a certain angle, it made you look pretty.

"You've never jumped in a well," I said.

"If Jugni told you that story, you would have completely believed her."

"This is true."

"Even if you knew she was lying."

"Even if I knew she was lying."

"That is so fucked-up. That's like larceny. That's how communism starts."

•

We made a plan.

1. Make a cunning lasso with the rope.
2. Capture the body in said cunning lasso.
3. Haul the bitch up.

There was only one of her and two of us so logically speaking, it should have been easy. But she was obscenely heavy for one woman and I remarked that it was like she had turned into three fat men after dying.

"That's totally something she would do," said Azhagu. "Especially if she knew you and I were hauling her up. She would definitely do that on purpose."

We decided to take a break. The sky was a dirty orange and the coconut trees stood out like black slashes against the sky. Jugni had always been distrustful of trees. Whenever we passed one, she made it a point to spit on it.

Imagine that, ladies. Imagine being so big you didn't have to care about someone spitting on you.

"You know what I really hate," said Azhagu. "I hate the whole Jugni thing. I mean that wasn't even her name. Her name was Rajalakshmi."

"Jugni said that a name was really just a number that had letters instead of numbers."

"And I hated that whole—" Azhagu tried to shake her hips.

"The what? The dancing?"

"She was a slut!"

"We're all sluts."

"And I hate how she kept using the eff word for everything. Everything was fuck. Fuck fuck fuck, fuck this, fuck that, fuck me, *Azhagu you are a fucking cunt.*"

"Oh yeah."

"You remember that? You remember when she said that?"

"I loved the way she said 'cunt'. The word automatically became a knife. You know?"

We went back to hauling the body up. Water flowed from the head and arms, echoing harshly against the walls of the well.

"Chee," said Azhagu with disgust. "Why does it have to be so loud?"

"It's acoustics or something. I don't really know."

"It's annoying."

"I was thinking of setting up a typing institute for young women with polio."

Azhagu stared at me, water dripping from her whitened knuckles.

"Right now?" she said.

"Not *right* now. When this is over."

"I didn't know you could type."

"I can't. But I feel I should do something for women with polio. Jugni always said that women with polio were like dolls that had their joints on the outside instead of the inside."

"She was a tireless advocate for the perpetuation of tuberculosis in women. Tireless."

"Yes, but I think she appreciated the physical aesthetics of polio a little more."

•

We draped the body over the edge of the well.

Ladies, when you die or faint or feel it must be the absolute end, arch your back. Nobody can question you. People will become incensed and then, in keeping with social norms, they will start to cry.

Water ran steadily through the thick, black hair, trickling along the lips which had peeled back to reveal a set of surprisingly yellow teeth.

"This isn't her," I said.

"You know that's just what I was thinking," said Azhagu. "I was thinking this isn't her. It's just not."

I thought of my shoulders and neck and how they were going to hurt because they weren't used to such excessive physical strain. I tried to remember if Jugni had ever said anything about physical strain. Once she made us study the waist of a woman who was carrying rocks on her head.

Note the curve ladies. Poverty tones the body naturally and in a completely healthy way. No additives, preservatives or artificial anythings.

I didn't think this physical strain was like poverty. But then again we no longer had the directions, we no longer had the camera, we hadn't recorded anything and apparently we didn't have Jugni's body either. We no longer *had*. So maybe it was like poverty only not in a mainstream way. Maybe it was unpoverty.

I looked at the woman's fingernails and the edge of her sari. Her face had been bruised, probably by the fall. Azhagu gave the body a strong push. It battered against the black-lichened walls, making the powder-blue crabs scurry for cover. When it hit the bottom, water seemed to explode all around it.

"Chee," said Azhagu. "So loud. Why does it have to be so loud?"

If I looked closely,
I could see that everything had changed.

Even his towels looked different
and I couldn't understand where they had come from
or why they were there.

But if I took a step back,
everything looked exactly the same.

the underground
bird sanctuary

Kathir's bones were pushing up under his skin like silent hills. His shoulders and wrists had knots of bones that were knuckling up so fiercely, it looked like they were going to break through. In the afternoons, I would count them while he tried to sleep.

"You're counting the same one twice," he would mumble without opening his eyes.

"Well it's poking up in two places. A lot of them are."

I was sure that some of them had already broken through his skin. Sometimes I would slip my hands under the back of his shirt, expecting his spinal column to fall through my fingers like a shower of boney coins. I was always a little surprised when this didn't happen.

Kathir was angry and disappointed in everything and I believed this was what made his bones so rebellious. He wanted to join the Naxalites, mainly because he had heard that one of his uncles had done this as a teenager. Unfortunately, he couldn't find any Naxalites and he didn't know where to look for them. He was here, in this small, crumpled town because it contained a few LTTE supporters and that was about as close to the Naxalites as he could get. Whenever someone asked Kathir what he did, he would say that he was doing everything. He was rehabilitating poor people even if they didn't want to be rehabilitated. He was saving broken animals, traditional Indian art forms and all the indigenous strains of rice that were being wiped out by American hybrids. He liked to say that he was not like the rest of us, because the rest of us did nothing. The rest of us always made Kathir angry. He would shame our jobs and educational qualifications, insult our families. Sometimes he would hit someone but usually, he ended up getting hit. Drunk and embarrassed men would carry him home, prop him up on the nearest plastic chair and say good night like they couldn't understand what I was doing in this place, with him.

Kathir worked when he felt like it and spent the rest of his time reading literary magazines from America and writing poetry about dead animals. His body was pale and hollow, his cargo shorts hanging limply from hip bones that jutted out like sharp stones. His cheeks and chin were covered with an uneven, patchy beard that looked like an infection.

"You need to eat something baby," I'd say, tugging at the top of his shorts. "Don't be like this."

"What's the matter?" he'd say. "Don't you like skinny guys?"

"This is not skinny. This is an anorexic on crack."

"Look at you, talking all American. Say something else."

"You really need to eat something," I'd say, wrapping my arms around his waist. "Really."

The only thing that did not anger or disappoint Kathir was dying birds. He liked to bring them home and he liked to get upset about the fact that they were dying. His mouth would set in a weak line and his breath would come out so crookedly that it sounded like he was wheezing. He would over-feed, over-water and over-everything them until they died, their beaks slightly open like they were surprised at his suffocating love. Once they died, he would ask me to bury them. I would wrap the bodies first in cloth, then in newspaper, and bury them in the strip of ground behind Kathir's one-room house. The strip was full of finches, mynahs, coloured chicks, crows and a small paradise flycatcher, all buried in sloppy ditches topped off with tiny piles of broken brick and gravel. I called it the Underground Bird Sanctuary. Sometimes Kathir laughed at this but usually he didn't because he said it didn't make any sense.

For a while, I lived with Kathir, his plastic chairs and his comic book collection that he kept wrapped in layers of white cotton cloth inside a steel trunk. He had a guitar, an amplifier and a motorcycle which he cleaned and took for a spin once a week. He slept on the floor, ate twice a day and walked to wherever he needed to go. If I had extra money, we took the bus.

"You can't do this," people would tell me. "He's a fucking train wreck. You'll end up killing yourself."

"He just needs to eat something," I'd say. "He'll be okay."

Every so often, I tried to make him do normalman things like break coconuts or go out and buy something. When he did go out, he would come home late with no money and sometimes no shoes. One night, Kathir brought home a kitten that was covered in mud and panting, which alarmed me because dogs were the ones that were supposed to pant, not cats. It took all night for the kitten to die and when it did, there was nothing to wrap it in. We finally used one of Kathir's shirts, knotting the sleeves across it like an oversized bow on a present.

"Now I need a new shirt," he said, frowning at the tiny bundle.

We decided to take a bus to town the next morning, buy him a new shirt and then sit on the rocky beach and share a paper cone of peanuts before going back home. While we waited in the moist, heavy heat of the bus stand, I wondered if the kitten meant that the sanctuary was about to diversify. Maybe he would start bringing home dying monkeys, civet cats and those tiny black piglets that ran so desperately up and down the road. Maybe when we ran out of space outside, we would start burying the bodies inside.

I turned to Kathir and told him I needed to go to the bathroom.

"Here?" he said, raising his eyebrows. "You want to use a bus stand bathroom?"

"I really need to go," I said.

He shook his head and shrugged. I walked to the other side of the bus stand, bought a bottle of cold water and caught the third bus I saw. I wondered how long he would wait before he realized I was not coming back.

•

I lived in the city for the next six months. I took up content development work, slept on a bed and ate french fries whenever I wanted. People said they were glad I was back and that I was looking so much better now.

When I lived with Kathir, I used to dream of Naxalites. They had large, black moustaches and Spanish accents and I dreamed that they were digging up the Underground Bird Sanctuary and setting all the birds free. I would ask the Naxalites if Kathir could join them but they would always say no. Then I would chase them, asking them to please reconsider but they would just keep running and shaking their heads. After I left Kathir, I started dreaming of birds. I dreamed that my arm was splitting open like a fish cutting through water and there were ravens, small eagles and sparrows gnarled and twisted around my bones. They fell out with a heavy sound, like wet cloth hitting the ground. The dead ones just lay there, their runny eyes staring at the birds that were still alive. The live ones would pick themselves up, shake out their wings and walk away.

Sometimes parts of Kathir's body would fall out along with the birds. Once his hand fell out, sliced cleanly at the wrist, clutching a tiny purple chick. Another time his entire torso spilled out, speckled with beaks and feathers. Sometimes his mouth would fall out and I would find a small finch nestled underneath his tongue.

One day, I called Kathir.

"I've been dreaming about you," I said. "You and the birds."

"What birds?" he said. His voice sounded slightly unfamiliar, like a shoe on the wrong foot.

"The Underground Bird Sanctuary," I said. "Remember? Your birds?"

"They aren't my birds."

"Well, no. They aren't anyone's birds I guess."

I asked if I could come down and see him and he said no. A couple of weeks later, I asked him again and he said yes.

•

Kathir would not meet me at the bus stand because of what I had done to him last time. Instead, he waited for me near a tiny shop where we used to buy green bananas. He was clean-shaven except for a stern moustache that curled up slightly at the ends. His hair was neatly trimmed and combed. He was wearing a pair of dark blue trousers and a white button-down shirt that was untucked, making him look uncannily like one of the local men. He looked at my bag but did not offer to carry it.

"So what's all this?" I asked. This was the first time I had seen him wearing something that wasn't baggy shorts or jeans.

"They're pants," he said.

"Are they new? They look new."

"No," he said as he started walking. "They're not new."

At home, we ate biriyani that tasted stale and oily. Kathir took his shirt off and spread a plastic bag on his lap so he wouldn't get his trousers dirty. He ate quietly and industriously, placing all the chicken bones and boiled egg white in neat piles at the side of his plate. I looked at his jaw, the swell of his arms and chest, the curve of his thumb. His bones seemed to have submerged completely inside his body. He was a stretch of gentle undulations now.

Kathir was no longer into dying birds. When I asked him why, he said things like "rabies" or "bird flu". I asked if he would buy me a black molly fish to keep and he said fish made him nervous.

"Besides," he said. "It's just for a few days."

"I didn't know fish made you nervous," I said.

"Well now you know."

That night I dreamed I was holding a live bird between my teeth. I couldn't see it but I knew I had caught it violently, with a hammer or a whip. Its feathers were slipping between the gaps of my teeth and sinking into my gums. Wake up, I told myself. Wake up now. I heard a tiny crack as my teeth punctured its skull and its brain spilled over into my mouth.

•

When I woke up the next morning, Kathir was already gone. He had left me a stack of mouldering English novels to read because there was nothing else to do there. I had leftover biriyani for breakfast and lunch and spent the day looking at his clothes, his bed sheets, the things he kept in the kitchen. If I looked closely, I could see that everything had changed. Even his towels looked different and I couldn't understand where they had come from or why they were there. But if I took a step back, everything looked exactly the same.

In the evening, we both walked to the nearby ice cream parlour and had orange ice sticks. I told him about my dream and the birds that spilled out of my arm. Kathir said a gang of monkeys lived in a nearby cell phone tower and kept opening taps and draining people's water tanks. He said that if he had a gun, he would shoot them.

"No, you wouldn't," I said.

"Yes, I would. You don't know," he said. He started chewing on the wooden ice stick, making a grating noise that was surprisingly loud.

"Do you have a gun?" I asked.

I waited as he chewed on the stick some more and then tossed it to the side of the road. But he didn't say anything.

A few days later, the stack of English novels was gone and I couldn't find anything to eat. When Kathir came back in the evening, we didn't go for orange sticks. Instead, we walked to the railway station and looked at train timings.

"There's one tomorrow morning, at 8," he said. "And another at 11. And then at 3. After that only at 9 so maybe—"

"What are you doing?" I said.

"You can take a train, trains are comfortable," he said, scribbling down letters and numbers on the back of an old receipt. "You won't be tired when you reach."

"But why?"

"What do you mean, why?"

"Why do you want me to take a train?" I said.

Kathir stared at me and it looked like his eyes had turned into marbles, shimmering under a skin of water. Once I had told him that his eyes were like chocolate and he had laughed and said nothing about my eyes, even after I had asked him to.

"So what do you want to do then?" he said.

"About what?"

We walked back home and Kathir would not speak to me for the rest of the night.

•

Kathir did not go out the next day. He brought me coffee, vadai and pongal for breakfast along with a newspaper. Then he said there was a bird sanctuary a few hours away, a real one, above ground and he laughed in a sparse, sharp-cornered way that reminded me of how his collarbone used to jut out of his chest. Two buses, he said. He pulled out an old travel bag and packed a bottle of water, two hats and the newspaper. He told me to bring my stuff, just in case, but he didn't say in case of what.

The first bus was crowded. Kathir was forced to sit at the very edge of our seat with his arm around my shoulders so he wouldn't fall off. Kathir started talking to a man who had a broken arm, saying that he had broken his arm too even though I was pretty sure he hadn't.

We got off at a small bus stand that consisted of a few pillars plastered with movie posters from two years ago. The righteous anger on the hero's face was fading to yellow while the heroine's face had already disappeared completely. A small tea stall leaned precariously to the left, threatening to keel over at any moment. Hidden in the depths of its thin shelves, I could see bottles of discontinued cola and dusty packages of biscuits. Kathir bought me a bottle of warm Bovonto and insisted I put it in my bag.

While we waited for the bus, he talked about the bird sanctuary and how he wished he had a camera. Then he talked about the monkeys in the cell phone tower and how people were throwing firecrackers at them now and it seemed to work, though some monkeys were getting singed but that didn't really matter because it was just monkeys.

"I thought of making a sign once," he said. "You know, for the yard. Underground Bird Sanctuary. I thought of taking a printout."

"You got a printer?"

"No but the guy at the Xerox shop said I could take one for free."

"Sometimes they charge seven bucks for a printout."

"Yeah. Or I thought maybe I'd just write it out in pen or something."

I nodded and looked at his wrists. They were heavy and rectangular now, like blocks of wood, completely free of bones.

Kathir told me to wait while he went to find out about the bus. I watched him walk away, the sunlight falling off his shoulders and pouring slowly down his back. And then he was gone.

I waited for him, the hero from the movie poster frozen with faded, yellow rage behind me. I waited and waited.

the four steps of standard plastination

1. Fixation

When Lily was born, it was decided she would be the last because the family already had too many children. She was named after her uncle's favorite song, "Lily Malar-ikku Kondattam". A year later, a runty, ill-tempered girl was born and named Inipothum, which means This Is Enough.

2. Dehydration

Right before Lily's aunt passed away, she told Lily not to do anything. *Don't run like a crazycrazy and tell everyone I'm dead. Do you understand? Do you understand what I'm saying?* Lily nodded and watched her aunt's eyes close, though they did not close completely. Then she went to the window and saw a boy called MaoZeTung sitting on a bench.

"Mousie," she called and he looked up.

"Come down," he said. "Come sit with me."

Lily looked over at her aunt, who was already stiffening on the bed. Then she told MaoZeTung to wait, she was coming.

3. Forced Impregnation In A Vacuum

Inipothum was on an athletics scholarship with a well-known women's college in the city. Lily had a speech impediment and thick strands of hair sprouting from her shoulders and the space between her breasts. She pulled these out with a tweezer and had nightmares about the black pits they left behind.

On the evening before she was scheduled to receive an award for Best Outgoing Student, Inipothum threw herself off a bridge. While her clothing was recovered, her body was never found. Lily thought of her sister lying at the bottom of the river, harboring tiny schools of fish inside her mouth. While thinking of this, she absentmindedly put a pencil in her ear and punctured her eardrum.

4. Hardening

After studying Ceramic Engineering in the North, MaoZeTung came back with a scanty beard and his lungs filled with tuberculosis. Whenever he coughed, his face would disappear into his spit bag and his shoulder blades shuddered under his shirt.

During the day, MaoZeTung made kites. In the evening, he flew them on the roof of his house while small, dusty children fluttered around his knees. Lily watched this and tugged at the hair between her breasts, though she didn't pull any out.

She calls me little niggerbitch.

She says hey little niggerbitch.

Stop walking on the snow, little niggerbitch.

go home, dallas

Before the tornado hit, the days were all the same. The mornings were slow and hot. The afternoons brimmed with dark thunderstorms that spat out pink lightning. Jai and I were not allowed outside because it was the summer of cigarettes and french kissing.

Every afternoon, Dallas would knock on our door and ask if she could come inside. When we said no, she would sit on our porch and tell us about her dad who lived across town in a house with a pool, how he had a Camaro, and how she was going to go live with him and have her own room.

"Camaros are stupid," said Jai, flicking tiny pebbles at her legs.

"He bought me a crimping iron, see?" said Dallas, holding up a bumpy shank of hair. "My dad says he saw a spinning cloud yesterday when it rained."

"Your Dad's stupid," said Jai.

Eventually our mother would tell Dallas to leave, and she would always walk away slowly, like her feet were heavy and there was nowhere to go. Sometimes she would stop and look back at us.

"Go home, Dallas," I would shout.

She would stand there for a while. Then she would turn around and go home.

•

The day before the tornado hit, people called the local radio station to talk about the spinning clouds they had seen. They wanted to know why they were spinning and if something bad was going to happen.

When Dallas came, she was wearing a red raincoat even though it wasn't raining. She had crimped all of her hair and burnt her eyelashes in the process.

"Look what I got, you guys," she said, pulling four hailstones from her pocket. They were the size of marbles and already melting into pools of dirty water.

"Let's see," said Jai, snatching them from her palm. He frowned at them and then began throwing them, one by one, as far as he could.

"Go fetch, Dallas!" he shouted before running into the house.

"I'm telling 'Ma," I called after him. Dallas was already across the street, pawing through the grass on her hands and knees.

"Found one!" she shouted, waving at me.

"Go home, Dallas," I shouted back. I watched her search some more and finally head home, empty-handed.

•

When the tornado hit, our dad was at work and our mother was out shopping. Hailstones the size of grapefruits smashed into the backyard. Jai ran in and out of the house, collecting hailstones in his t-shirt and dumping them into the freezer. Every so often, the hail would stop and everything would be clear and quiet.

It was during one of these lulls that Dallas came, carrying an umbrella and a lunch box.

"I brought cookies," she said. "Can I come in?"

"Go home, Dallas," I said, trying to close the door. "It's a real bad storm, you have to go home."

"I have my umbrella," she said, shaking it out. "See?"

"Go home, Dallas," said Jai before slamming the door in her face. Almost immediately, we heard the storm start again. We stood there, listening to the hailstones batter against the house. Finally Jai opened the door again, but she was gone.

"Dallas!" he shouted. "You idiot! Dallas!"

We called her name and tried to make out her tiny figure in the whirling shriek of the storm. We called her name until the storm shoved us back inside, soaking wet and bruised by the hail.

"She's probably home, right?" said Jai. He was already starting to shiver.

"Yeah," I said. "She's probably home."

•

When it was all over, Jai and I went to Dallas' house, carrying one of the huge hailstones he had collected from the storm. We went back three times before her mom answered the door and said that Dallas was busy and we should come back tomorrow. She wouldn't take the hailstone, even though Jai asked her twice. A couple of days later, Dallas went to live with her dad and we did not see her again. We kept her hailstone in the freezer for a long time. When we finally threw it in the sink, it took a long time to melt.

frostbite

Selvi's dad dunked her frostbitten feet into a pot of hot water and held them down, even after she started screaming. Selvi's brother kicked the wall and shouted, "You're supposed to use warm water for frostbite, you stupid fuck! You stupid Paki fuck!" His father yelled back at him in Tamil, blaming him for being born, for Selvi's frostbitten feet and for the fact that she had waited two hours in the snow in dress shoes. Selvi's brother kicked the pot of hot water over and ran out of the house. He caught a bus to the library and cried quietly in the geology section until it was closing time. When he got home, he helped his father clean up the mess in the kitchen.

"I used warm water after you left," his father said. "I think she'll be alright."

Selvi's brother said she would be fine, and it probably wasn't frostbite anyway.

•

On Saturday afternoon, Selvi's father took them to the Space Science Centre, bought them root beer and gave them each a quarter to spend on the candy machines. When they got home, he told them he had lost his job.

"So what's going to happen?" asked Selvi's brother.

"Nothing. We will cut the cable connection," said his father. "And sell the coffee table."

Selvi and her brother watched strangers come to their house and take away their stereo system, their living room furniture and the TV set. Their father stayed home all day and vacuumed the carpet in slow, straight lines. Selvi's brother started stealing books from the school library and hiding them under his bed. When Selvi's friends came home and asked if she was moving, she would say yes and promise to show them pictures of the new house because it had two garages and her room was totally massive and had a window seat.

•

Selvi's Language Arts journal was supposed to include rhyming poems and an essay on her summer vacation. Instead, she wrote poems that didn't rhyme about frostbite, the way her father's mouth looked when he was angry, and how her cold feet looked inside a pot of hot water. She also wrote one rhyming poem about her classmate Ryan Kowalchuk, whose name she rhymed with "suck" and "fuck".

"I spoke to your father," said Mrs. Pawluski, tapping Selvi's journal with a fat, waxy finger. "He thinks you did this because you were upset that he sold the TV. Is that true?"

"No," said Selvi.

"You want to tell me why you wrote these?"

"Can I have them back?"

"No."

Selvi was given her second warning of the year and one month's detention. This was increased to two months when she was caught circulating a poem about Mrs. Pawluski, which contained the phrases "fucking bitchski" and "sucks dickski".

•

Selvi's father discovered the stolen library books while vacuuming under his son's bed. When Selvi came home, she found him sitting on the floor, surrounded by outdated math textbooks, *Sweet Valley High* paperbacks, French-English dictionaries and an illustrated encyclopaedia of fairies. He looked small and smudged among the strong, sharp angles of the books.

"My son is a thief," he said quietly in Tamil. "My daughter writes filth in school and my son is a thief."

Selvi sat beside him and listened to the cars carve noisily through the slush in the streets. She looked at the furniture marks on the carpet. She could still see thick circles from where the sofa used to be. The marks from the coffee table had almost disappeared.

"I think we may have to sell the house," said her father.

"When?"

"Maybe after we sell the dining table."

When Selvi was younger, she would sometimes pretend that this was not her house and her father was not her father. He was just an uncle visiting from India and the house was someone else's entirely. They were sitting together simply by chance and in a few minutes, she would leave and never see him again.

Selvi's father tapped her on the shoulder.

"Come," he said, getting up. "He'll be home soon."

Her father took the heavier ones and Selvi took the paperbacks. Together, they carried the books back upstairs.

the gods in the basement

That was the year of prayer meetings. They met in people's basements and prayed in front of different gods while Anandhi picked at the carpet or traced the lines on her palm. When they started holding prayer meetings for Arul, she would sit very still and say "beebeebeebee" under her breath so it looked like she was praying. Sometimes she would close her eyes and say "Muay Thai" over and over again in quiet desperation. After each prayer meeting, someone passed around a plate of cookies and Anandhi wandered around the house, peering into closets and pocketing spare change she found on the dressers. That was the year Anandhi realized you could steal money after a prayer meeting, even when the gods were in the basement, and nothing would happen to you.

•

Back when Arul was eight and Anandhi was seven, they would skip Tamil classes at the Hindu community centre and sit at the bus stop, eating lint-covered cinnamon hearts and lying to each other about their lives. Now Arul was thirteen and in a coma because he had tried to kill himself. The last time Anandhi had seen him was at a prayer meeting for someone's grandmother. He had sat beside her, picking at the dry skin around his fingernails. Afterwards, they ate cookies together over the kitchen sink.

"Remember when I told you I went dirt biking every summer?" said Arul. "I lied. I never go anywhere in the summer."

"I'm going to Malibu in the summer," said Anandhi. "Me and my friends are going to be models."

"I've never been to Malibu."

"I went last summer, that's where this modelling agent saw me. I'm modelling for him. Me and my friends."

Arul nodded but didn't say anything. Then he said he was going to the bathroom and didn't come back. Anandhi wandered around the living room, pocketing a tiny wooden elephant, then hiding it in a potted plant.

That was the year it snowed in March. It was the year Arul left the prayer meeting early without saying goodbye, but when he saw Anandhi at the window he smiled at her and she smiled back.

•

That was also the year they had the most crowded prayer meeting. People stood on the stairs, rubbing their faces like something bad had already happened. While everyone sang a song about falling at the feet of God, a boy called Kumar slipped a piece of gum into Anandhi's hand.

"You can have two if you want," he whispered. "I got more."

Anandhi felt his cool, soft fingers against her palm as he pressed another stick into her hand.

"This is a prayer meeting," said Anandhi.

"So?"

"The guy's in the hospital, asshole," she said, shoving the gum back at him. "He could die."

"Sorry, bitch," said Kumar.

Afterwards, Anandhi wandered into the master bedroom and found a thick wad of dollar bills on the dresser. She counted them slowly—when Kumar appeared at the door and stood watching her, she counted them again and put them in her pocket.

"Hey come on," said Kumar. "Aunty works at Zellers, for Chrissake."

"Like I give a fuck."

"They shop at Fedco, man. Come on."

She took two notes, then one. Kumar would not take any. Finally she left the money on the dresser, told Kumar he was an asshole, and left.

•

That was the year Arul died and everyone said it was due to complications because no one wanted to say it was suicide. At the funeral, Anandhi noticed that the gods from the basement were propped up on chairs in the first row. They seemed small and bright, unaware of the boy stretched out in front of them, the bruises on his neck buried under flowers placed by people who were anxious to go back home. Some uncles talked about how well Arul did in school, how religious he was, but Anandhi had no idea who they were talking about.

That was the year they decided to hold future prayer meetings at the community centre. Arul was cremated, Anandhi turned twelve, and the gods went back to the basement.

the most beautiful woman in the world is calling me niggerbitch

We walked to school in wintercoats our mother had bought us from Fedco, each one puffed out in the colours of cheap insulation, hanging from our non-immigrant shoulders like garbage bags. We walked to school while our faces were sliced into shades of frostbite which my mother tried to fix with white clots of coconut oil that left us smelling rancid and foreign. My mother's face, brown as a nut, small and rich, wrapped in two scarves she got at dollarfortynine day. The snowflakes churning out of the dirty sky, the flurries which are different from a snowstorm, the scattered flurries like desiccated coconut shavings from the sky, the idea of each snowflake being different, that someone was up there making them. That we had no real idea if they really *were* all different, that we had no way of knowing if they were repeated every thousand years. We walked past the break in the apartments, the broken lamplight bleeding yellow on the snow and sickly trees, and then the most beautiful woman in the world. The most beautiful woman in the world leaning out of her window, her blonde hair dancing against her cheek, one hand on the window, her mouth open like a cut of pale pink in the sky, looking at us like a model from a Kmart flier showing off her sweater. The most beautiful woman in the world leaning down, stretching over us like the sky and shouting the word "niggerbitch" into air that is so shrivelled that it cannot contain her voice or her words. All it can do is tremble against her wisps of blonde hair and cover her with scattered flurries. My face turned up to the skanky snowflakes in the dirty sky, letting them tangle up in my face, my mom with her nutbrown hair, rich as a wintercoat, cutting through the cold air, brushing off the scattered flurries, telling me to don'tlookdon'tlistendon'tlook.

She calls me little niggerbitch. She says hey little niggerbitch. Stop walking on the snow, little niggerbitch. My mother's nutbrown face plows through the frosted air, snowflakes and tangle as she jerks me forward like she is sad that this is now my fault.

If the little niggerbitch can't walk on the snow and there is snow all over the ground, where should the little niggerbitch walk?

Basically the little niggerbitch can walk up the trees and along the top of the fence. She can walk in the air where it is not snowing. She can also stay at home because people can catch colds when they walk outside in the snow. Little niggerbitch can walk up the sides of buildings but not on top of them. She can walk above the inbetween clouds and on the edge of the sunset, on the backs of McDonald's seagulls. Little niggerbitch can follow the snow machines to the end of the road, where the road becomes nothing. She can go back to Africa or Pakiland or wherever the fuck niggerbitches come from, where it is hot all the time and everyone is poor. She can walk wherever she wants there, because there is no snow because people there don't even know what snow is.

The most beautiful woman in the world keeps saying niggerbitch until she can't see us anymore. She spatters our backs with her uncontainable words so we can take them home with us, so we have something to remember her by.

"Come on everyone," Moustachio said with a sigh.
"Let's get ready for Christmas Eve."

how juniper parsnip
saved christmas eve

Every evening, Juniper· Parsnip's family decorated their Christmas tree. They wrapped tinsel around it, going round and round until Juniper's brother Geranium got vertigo and had to lie down. Juniper's father Moustachio would fume and curse and sputter at the Christmas lights which never seemed to work properly. He would rant and rage and say all kinds of bad words until Juniper's mother Philomina made him go do yoga to calm down. Finally, Philomina would burn her Oh-So-Christmassy Christmas Eve Cookies and have a nervous breakdown behind the tree.

After all this happened, Juniper Parsnip would check on Geranium to make sure his vertigo hadn't made him fall off the bed. She would help her father untwist and uncurl himself from his calming yoga pose. And then she would convince her mother that the Oh-So-Christmassy Christmas Eve Cookies were awesome and that she should come out from behind the tree. This happened every single evening of Juniper Parsnip's life, whether it was summer or winter, rainy or snowy. This happened because in Ampersandulum, where the Parsnips lived, it was always Christmas Eve.

The reason for this could be found in Ampersandulum's Town Square, where a statue called The Great Stone Calendar stood as big as a bus and as grey as a storm cloud. It was a huge statue of a tear-away desk calendar commissioned many years ago by Calendaria, one of Ampersandulum's founders. Calendaria was a tiny woman with white hair that was so long she used it as a bed sheet. She loved calendars because they reminded people that time passes. Today became tomorrow very quickly. And before you knew it, next week became last year and three years ago soon became so long ago that nobody could even remember it happening. Calendars were a way of reminding you how important Now was because very soon, Now became Then.

Legend has it that Calendaria had originally wanted the calendar to say,

Do it Now,
Before Now
Becomes Then.

But when the statue arrived, it was discovered that "December 24th" was cut grimly and darkly into the calendar face. There were rumours that this had been done by subversive groups who did not like doing anything Now or Then or Ever. Calendaria became very sick and kept muttering, "How will the date change? How can Christmas Eve become Christmas if the date doesn't change?" She looked at The Great Stone Calendar every single day and the hopelessness of it caused her to waste away until all that was left of her was her long, white hair.

After that, things in Ampersandulum changed very quickly. A law was passed, stating that Christmas Eve would be celebrated every day until the date on The Great Stone Calendar changed. Declarations, petitions, constitutions, proclamations, instigations and celebrations were held so that nobody had a moment to question the absurdity of this idea.

In the beginning, everybody liked celebrating Christmas Eve every day. It was fun to decorate the tree, put presents under it and have friends and family over for a Traditional Ampersandulum Christmas Eve Turkey Dinner. But soon, it started getting boring. And then it started getting irritating. People had to buy Christmas turkeys every day and soon there were no turkeys left in Ampersandulum. The Christmas trees started to die and the plastic ones started to break so people had to keep buying new ones. Meeting the same friends and family over and over again made a lot of people argue and fight with each other. People had to visit Holiday

Violence Therapists to make sure they celebrated Christmas Eve without killing each other. People also had to hire storage units for their growing piles of presents. Children watched with dismay as the pile of unopened gifts under the tree grew larger and larger each day. Soon those children grew into adults who no longer cared about these Christmas gifts. They no longer cared about the Christmas tree or Christmas dinner. In fact, they no longer cared about Christmas because in Ampersandulum, Christmas never came. It was always and forever Christmas Eve.

Some people loved Everyday Christmas Eve though. The companies who sold Completely Instant, Completely Artificial Traditional Ampersandulum Christmas Eve Turkey Dinners loved it. So did the Christmas tree businesses, the shopping malls, the Holiday Violence Therapists, the wrapping paper businesses and the gift storage facilities. They all loved Everyday Christmas Eve because they were making lots and lots and lots of money because of it.

Each morning, Juniper and her family walked to the centre of Ampersandulum to see if The Great Stone Calendar had changed. There, they would see hundreds of other children with their parents, looking at the calendar and sighing because it was still December 24th.

"Come on everyone," Moustachio would say with a sigh. "Let's get ready for Christmas Eve."

And they would all walk slowly and sadly home. One day, Juniper looked at her father and noticed how stressed and crooked he was from the calming yoga poses. She looked at her brother who walked in a wobbly line because of his frequent vertigo attacks. She looked at her mother who was already doing deep-breathing exercises to calm herself for the inevitable breakdown that would happen that evening.

"I hate Everyday Christmas Eve," Juniper said softly, taking her father's hand.

"I do too," said her father.

•

In an effort to keep up with the rising demand for Christmas trees, a company began selling Fabulously Fuzzy Christmas WonderTrees, which were in fact just sticks covered in fuzzy green fungus and glitter. Moustachio brought one of these trees home and in exactly twenty minutes, the entire Parsnip family had Acute Fuzzy Fungal Fever. For the next three days, they sniffled and coughed and ached and made nourishing soups for each other. For three days they did not decorate the tree or have Christmas Eve dinner or do anything that was even remotely Christmassy. It was the best three days the Parsnips ever had.

But on the fourth day, when they were better, the Parsnips had to make their way again to the Town Square to see if The Great Stone Calendar had changed. It hadn't. And as they walked home sadly and slowly, Juniper began to think. She thought about how they hadn't celebrated Christmas Eve for three whole days and the calendar hadn't changed and everything was just as it had always been. The Parsnips hadn't celebrated for three whole days and it hadn't made a difference.

That evening, when Juniper was helping her dad untangle himself from his calming yoga pose, she told him about what she had been thinking. Moustachio started thinking about this too and in the middle of the night, he woke his wife and told her about it. In the morning, the Parsnips held a secret family conference. It was decided that they would no longer celebrate Everyday Christmas Eve. On the outside, they would have to make it seem like they were celebrating just like everyone else. But at home, where no one could see them, there would be no tree decorating or gifts or Christmas turkeys or anything. It was the most brilliant idea ever! The entire Parsnip family jumped up and down as quietly as they could so the neighbors couldn't hear them. They had never been so happy since they all got sick.

For a while, the Parsnips were indeed the happiest family in all of Ampersandulum. There was a spring in their step when they walked over to the Town Square to see that the calendar hadn't changed. Geranium's vertigo disappeared completely and he was now able to devote more time to his new hobby of tightrope walking. Philomina no longer had nervous breakdowns and began spending her time composing symphonies. Moustachio was so calm that he was able to focus on developing his yoga and levitation skills. Now, Juniper happily spent her evenings watching her brother tightrope walking across the ceiling while her father levitated in a corner and her mother hummed along with the symphony she was composing.

But unfortunately, the Parsnip family was being watched. Reports were coming into the Great Government Office that the Parsnips had only bought one tree and one Completely Instant, Completely Artificial Traditional Ampersandulum Christmas Eve Turkey Dinner all month. They had bought no tinsel, no wrapping paper and they hadn't visited their Holiday Violence Therapists at all. It was clear that the Parsnips had been indulging in anti-Everyday Christmas Eve activities of the worst kind.

"Oh dear," muttered the Accountant of Everyday Christmas Eve Accountability as he frowned over the numbers. "This won't do. This won't do at all."

He issued an order to have the entire Parsnip family arrested for Anti-Everyday Christmas Eve activities. Furthermore, they would have their day in court after which they would be found guilty and sent to make artificial Christmas trees in the Dark Mountains.

"Imagine that. Not celebrating Christmas Eve every day!" muttered the Accountant. "No, that simply won't do at all."

•

The arrest of the entire Parsnip family caused a sensation in Ampersandulum. People accused of Anti-Everyday Christmas Eve activities were usually whisked away in the middle of the night and never heard from again. But in this case, the Government wanted to make an example of the Parsnips. They wanted everyone to see what a terrible thing they had done and they wanted everyone to understand that if they didn't celebrate Christmas Eve every day, they would be punished too.

But as soon as news of the arrest was released, an underground group called the Anti-Everyday Christmas Eve Brigade began plastering Ampersandulum with posters, demanding that the Parsnips be set free and that the celebration of Christmas Eve every day be stopped. The Government took all these posters down and a few hours later, more posters appeared. Anti-Everyday Christmas Eve pirate radio stations popped up and began broadcasting all over Ampersandulum. Anti-Everyday Christmas Eve songs were composed and sung at secret Anti-Everyday Christmas Eve rallies. It seemed like the Anti-Everyday Christmas Eve sentiment was far stronger and more widespread than the Government had anticipated. The Accountant of Everyday Christmas Eve Accountability was so irritated that he starting getting ulcers and acidity.

"It's Ungovernmental! Unconstitutional! Unpermissable! Unprofessional!" he sputtered. "It just won't do. It won't do at all!"

Arrangements were made to immediately hold an open court in Ampersandulum's Town Square, right next to The Great Stone Calendar. The Parsnip family would be tried, found guilty and exiled as soon as possible. The sooner this was done, the sooner the Anti-Everyday Christmas Eve sentiment would die down and Ampersandulum could go back to business as usual.

On the day of the trial, the Town Square was packed. Some people were brave enough to hold signs that said FREE THE PARSNIPS! BAN EVERYDAY CHRISTMAS EVE! Others just stood there silently, wondering what would happen to the Parsnip family. The Parsnips themselves were in bad shape. Moustachio had twisted himself into such a complicated calming yoga pose that he couldn't get untwisted. Geranium's vertigo was so bad that he was continuously falling down. Philomena was having her largest nervous breakdown on record, insisting she was perfectly alright while refusing to come out from under the bed. The only person who seemed to be okay was little Juniper. But deep down, Juniper wasn't okay at all. She was very scared about going on trial and going to the Dark Mountains and seeing her family in such a mess.

"You've got to do it Juniper," her father's voice drifted up through a tangle of arms and legs. "You've got to defend the Parsnips in court."

"But what can I do? I'm too little! I'm just a little girl," said Juniper.

"You're Juniper Parsnip," said her mother from under the bed. "You're Juniper Parsnip and that means you're not just a little girl. You're special. You can do things that nobody else can do."

"But what? How am I special? What can I do?" asked Juniper. She felt that if she knew this, she would feel a lot better about going to court by herself. But before anyone could answer her, the guards came to take her to the Town Square.

"Good luck Juniper! You can do it," shouted Geranium, followed by a crash as he fell down. As Juniper walked past the other jail cells, she heard other people tell her the same thing.

"Good luck Juniper Parsnip!"

"Go get 'em, Juniper Parsnip!"

"You can do it, Juniper Parsnip!"

Juniper did not feel better hearing these words. She started to feel worse! What were these people talking about? She was just a little girl! How could she do anything against a big government in a big court? They had her mixed up with someone else. Either that or everyone had gone crazy.

Soon Juniper found herself standing in the Town Square, surrounded by a large crowd of people. A huge judge's bench loomed in front of her. It was so big that she couldn't even see the Accountant of Everyday Christmas Eve Accountability who was sitting behind it, muttering and mumbling and coughing in a very important way. Juniper had never felt so small in her entire life. *He can't even see me,* she thought to herself. *I'm too little. How can anyone see me? How can I do anything if no one can even see me?*

Juniper also noticed that for the first time in her life, she could see The Great Stone Calendar up close. She was surprised to see that it was filled with tiny cracks and in some places, small chunks of the stone had fallen away. Something shiny and purple was peeking out from underneath. It was almost as if something was hidden under the stone—but no, that was just silly, Juniper told herself.

"Order, order," boomed the voice of the Accountant of Everyday Christmas Eve Accountability from somewhere above her. "Let the first offence against the Parsnip family be duly noted, the offence being wrongful representation by a small girl."

"What's so wrongful about that?" blurted out Juniper before she could stop herself.

"Small girls aren't even supposed to be in court, you silly. Why isn't your father here?"

"He's sick. My whole family is sick because of Everyday Christmas Eve."

A rumble passed through the spectators crowded in the Town Square. "Everyday Christmas Eve makes me sick too!" someone shouted.

"See?" thundered the booming voice. "You see what you and your family have done? Why, it's Anarchy! Communism! Secularism! Terrorism! Do you see what ruination you and your family have caused?"

Juniper didn't see any of this because Juniper wasn't even paying attention to what the booming voice was saying. She was too busy looking at the calendar. She noticed that whenever the crowd of spectators rumbled or murmured, or whenever the booming voice boomed, bigger cracks appeared in the stone surface. More chunks had fallen off the sides and corner of the calendar.

"Are you listening to me? You! Down there! Are you listening?" said the booming voice.

"Hmm?" said Juniper. *It's because of the noise*, she thought. *I don't think there's ever been this much noise next to the calendar before and it's making all the cracks bigger. And there is something purple underneath, I can see it! I wonder what would happen if...*

"If I plead guilty, can I ask for one last request from the court?" asked Juniper suddenly.

"You have already been found guilty," said the booming voice. "But yes, since you're a small girl, you may ask a favor. Would you like a doll? A frilly pink dress? A cupcake?"

"I'd like everyone here to sing 'We Wish You a Merry Christmas'."

"Very patriotic of you. The court approves."

The crowd began to rumble again, this time with dismay. The poor little girl had given in. She had lost. What did you expect, some people said, she's just a little girl.

"Don't do it Juniper! Don't give up!" someone called from the crowd.

"Come on, let's sing really loud," said Juniper. "Let's sing as loud as we can."

They all thought of poor Juniper and her poor family who were going to be heading to the Dark Mountains to make Christmas trees for the rest of their lives. Everyone started to sing, first halfheartedly but then with more and more feeling as more voices joined in. The booming voice joined in too. Juniper sang as loud as she could. She shut her eyes and sang so loud that she couldn't even hear herself. She was sure that she had never sung so loud in her whole life.

Suddenly there was a loud, deafening crack. Everyone stopped singing and a gasp of surprise shot through the crowd.

The Great Stone Calendar was falling to pieces right before their eyes!

It was cracking and crumbling into a tired grey heap of dust. And out of the heap appeared a bright shiny purple tablet with the sparkly words

Do it Now,
Before Now
Becomes Then.

Underneath these words was a set of numbers. Juniper saw it was a calendar that had been keeping the date all these years under the stone surface.

Everyone started cheering and crying and laughing. "December 24th" had vanished from The Great Stone Calendar! Everyday Christmas Eve was finally over! The booming voice was so busy trying to quell the rebellion that was quickly spreading through the crowd that it didn't notice little Juniper had climbed on top of the big judge's bench.

"Hey everyone!" she shouted. "It's October 2nd. Look at the calendar. It says October 2nd."

The crowd stared at her in stunned silence. They were trying to remember what those words meant. October. October 2nd. October.

"Why, it's my birthday," said an old man near the front.

"It's my wedding anniversary tomorrow!"

"I have to go back to class!"

"I have to go on vacation!"

Suddenly everyone remembered what they had to do and where they had to go. There was a giant stampede as people joyfully went off to do all the things they had to do on October 2nd. Soon, the Town Square was empty. Juniper began climbing down from the judge's bench.

"Where do you think you're going?" said the booming voice. Juniper turned to look at the Accountant of Everyday Christmas Eve Accountability. She was surprised to see that he was actually a very small man, no bigger than she was. "You and your family have to go to the Dark Mountains," he said. "You have to celebrate Christmas Eve every day!"

"No we don't," said Juniper as she jumped to the ground. "You know why? Because it's not Christmas Eve. It's October 2nd. Christmas Eve is on December 24th and that's when we will celebrate it. After that, we will celebrate Christmas. And that will be all the Christmas we will have for the whole year. Now if you'll excuse me, I'm going to get my family out of jail. And then we're going home and we're going to take down our Christmas tree."

•

It took a while for Ampersandulum to fully shake off all those years of Everyday Christmas Eve celebrations. People emptied out their gift storage units and were overjoyed at some of the gifts they got but sad because now they had outgrown most of them. The gift storage facilities went out of business almost overnight. The Holiday Therapists lost all their clients because everyone was unstressed and happy that they didn't have to celebrate Christmas Eve every day. It would take a while before the trees and turkeys came back to Ampersandulum. But for now, everyone was just very happy not to celebrate Christmas Eve every day. They were happy doing all the big things, little things, ordinary things, extraordinary things, serious things, silly things and all those everyday things that they had almost forgotten about.

For the first time ever, life became normal for the Parsnip family. Juniper discovered that she was very interested in acoustics and decided that she wanted to do research in acoustical engineering and architecture when she was older. And when December finally made its way to Ampersandulum, she found that she was actually looking forward to celebrating Christmas Eve. In fact, for the first time in a long time, everyone in Ampersandulum was looking forward to Christmas Eve. They looked forward to seeing their friends and family, buying presents and having a Traditional Ampersandulum Christmas Eve Turkey Dinner. More importantly, everyone was looking forward to Christmas Eve finally turning into Christmas Day.

After all, when Christmas Eve comes around just once a year, that's something special. It's something worth celebrating.

We decide that he must be wailing through his nose, and that this must be something dragons can do which most people don't know about.

pazhani

A bus finally lurches into view at 6:30 a.m. with the word PAZHANI written on the front in Tamil and English. On the side, in large cursive letters, are the words DVD HAI SANGEETHA. The song "Marugo Marugo" is crashing through the speakers, sprinkled with only a small cloud of static. There are empty seats. There is even a TV. Uncle inspects the front of the bus, the driver, and the conductor. Then he walks back to where my sister and I are anxiously waiting beside a pile of faded bricks.

"Can we get in?" asks S. "Please?"

"Private buses best avoided," says Uncle. "And these young fellows are such rascal drivers."

"But there are seats!" I say. "We can sit down! In the seats!"

"We'll catch the 6:30 government bus. That will also have seats."

The 6:30 government bus arrives at 7:30, stuffed with grim women with large handbags, school children, vegetable vendors and drunken men who have tried to prop their faces against the windows. Uncle steps into the road and puts his arm straight out, in again and then out. It looks like he is trying to cut a slice of the morning air.

"Oh my God, what is he doing?" says S. "Why is he doing that?"

The bus stops and the driver shouts something which we can't understand, though we have a feeling it isn't very nice.

"Come come," says Uncle, steering us towards the door.

"There are no seats…" says S nervously.

"There are always seats," he says.

We stumble among starched saris and angry elbows until we are suddenly sitting next to a woman who says "sit sit sit sit" to us, even after we have sat down. The bus starts to move. We watch some people fight in the neighbouring seat and then we look out the window. Cows gaze thoughtfully into the peach blush of the morning while people stand outside their houses and brush their teeth. Every so often we see sleepy men sitting importantly in plastic chairs at the side of the road. Everything is cool and a little smoky.

"The other bus would have been nice, no?" I say as we stare at a group of children who are jumping up and down and waving.

"Yeah," says S. "I like listening to 'Marugo Marugo' in the bus."

•

Until yesterday, my sister and I had been spending our holidays at Uncle's house, reading his old books and looking at his perpetually sleeping dog. While our mother and aunt sorted through ancestral property issues, we had read *Karma Cola* three times and wondered if the sleeping dog was actually dead. One evening during a power cut, Uncle spoke to us about his new compost heap in the backyard, the degradation of morality in Indian politics, and Pazhani.

"I have not visited Pazhani in very long," he said through the hum of the mosquitoes. "I should very much like to go."

"Why?" I asked, waving my hands around my ears.

"Why not? You both should come. Youngsters shouldn't stay inside all the time."

"But we don't like buses," said my sister.

"Who likes buses? Buses are buses," he said.

"It will be hot," I ventured.

"Be ready by 5:30," he said, slapping his arms. "We will go."

"5:30 in the morning?"

The lights flickered on and Uncle got up, clapping his hands.

"See? It's an auspicious sign," he said.

"Are we going by bus?" I asked anxiously.

"Why think about the bus? Think about Pazhani."

We watched him disappear into the hallway and then the power went again. The heavy chorus of mosquitoes picked up where it had left off.

"I think that means we're going by bus," said S.

•

When we reach Pazhani, the cool, peach-coloured morning has peeled back into a dry, hot day. We watch Uncle drink his fourth cup of tea and assure him that we don't want any ComplanHorlicks, not even milk. He carefully inspects two bottles of water before he buys them and puts them in his yellow cloth bag.

"You can walk, no?" he says. "To the top?"

"Yeah, no problem."

"693 steps. You can walk?"

"We can walk," we say, because for some reason, 693 does not seem like a lot of steps when you are young and feel like you can do anything.

"Ropecar is there," says Uncle.

An old woman, who seems to be folded in two, shuffles past us towards the first flight of steps.

"We can walk," we say. "No problem."

After the first flight of steps S decides to take it slow. She lags two steps behind Uncle and says she doesn't want to talk while climbing. Uncle takes brisk but measured steps, stopping at each landing to stretch and shake out his legs. I climb the steps easily and believe that I will be at the top in about 10 minutes. I fall in step with Uncle and he greets me like he is seeing me for the first time.

"Why did you like coming here?" I ask.

"Why do you like staying at home?" he says.

"I don't. I just don't like travelling. I don't like the buses and heat."

"That is not travelling. That is just buses and heat."

"Are we almost there?" I ask, suddenly aware of the heaviness in my legs. Uncle looks at me in surprise.

"Nononono, still much farther to go. You are tired?"

"No," I say. I lag behind Uncle, then S. Then I start writing letters to God.

Dear Pazhani God, I think my legs are going to fall off. Please make the top come soon. Also I can't breathe and there are old people going up past me and this doesn't seem fair.

At some point, Uncle goes to the side, sits down and takes out a bottle of water. I collapse beside him while S trots ahead a bit and then comes back to join us.

"You wore yourself out," she says to me.

"No."

"We're not even halfway up."

"I'm fine."

"And then we need to walk all the way down."

I ignore her and take a long drink of warm water.

Dear Pazhani God, thank you for letting us sit down. Also if the top doesn't come soon and my legs do fall off, I feel that will be your fault.

•

When we reach the top, I keep asking Uncle if we have reached the top and we momentarily lose my sister in the crowd. When we are ushered into a bustling line, he suddenly turns around and says "Look! Look!" I turn one way and get an eyeful of elbows. I turn the other way and see something golden, some flowers and then I am outside again.

And I am unbelievably happy. I'm not sure why—it could be because I have made it to the top and my legs haven't fallen off. A woman comes forward, smiles, and puts something cool on my forehead. I smile back at her. I want to tell her that I almost spent this day sitting at my uncle's place reading *Karma Cola* for the gazillionth time and wondering if his dog was dead. But instead I am here and it is the best thing in the world. I want to tell her everything that has happened today and then I see the tray poking into my chest, the small picture of a God obscured by streaks of sandalwood and vibuthi, the coins.

"You want *money*?" I say. "You're not happy that I'm happy? You just want money?"

Uncle steers S and I into a corner where we sit and eat Marie biscuits. People around us rearrange their bags, stretch out and sleep.

"I can't believe she wanted money," I say as I hand the biscuit packet back to Uncle.

"Why focus on that?" he says. "Anyway, they also have to make money, no?"

"Is it easier going down?" I ask.

"Little easier," says Uncle. "But only a little."

•

On the way down we walk single file, S first, Uncle, then me. The day has begun to cool and by the time we reach the bottom, the shadows are longer and the evening lights and smoke have started to rise from the street. We walk to a hotel where Uncle orders idli-vadai and tea for himself and samosas for us. He also orders two bottles of Coca-Cola.

"Don't tell your mother," he says.

We eat slowly, talking about the monsoons and the many ways in which the Southern Railways can be improved. Then we walk to the bus stand, passing hawkers selling colourful piles of underwear, paper-thin handkerchiefs and plastic cricket bats. We manage to catch a straight bus home. We even get a seat. Uncle sits at the edge, arms crossed, his bag sitting snugly between his feet.

"Tomorrow rest," he says. "Your legs will be quite paining tomorrow. Then day after we will go to Madurai, Athens of East. Athens of ?"

"East," we say.

"Also home of the famous Madurai Meenakshi Temple," he says, settling back into the seat.

"Are we going by bus?" asks S.

"Yes," he says and closes his eyes. We watch his face relax as he falls asleep. Then we look out the window and watch lights wink to life in the distance as the sky slowly darkens.

"Maybe he'll buy us Coke again," I say.

"Maybe," says S.

boys like that

Boys like that start out with an eighteen percent chance of survival. They are born in the evening, arriving in bodies that are too small for their skin. Runny foods are spooned into their mouths because it is the right thing to do. Hard young aunts and uncles look at boys like that, cross their arms, and wait for them to die. When they don't die, it is not considered a miracle because the doctor will say that sometimes things like this happen, sometimes boys like that live. For many years afterwards, when people think of boys like that, they will think of leaks in the ceiling that can never be fixed, persistent blooms of black mould and old people that take a very long time to die.

•

Boys like that are ugly babies. They smile at everyone and offer wilted flowers to tables and plastic chairs. Nobody picks them up unless it is an absolute emergency. In this way, boys like that learn to love hairballs, shoes, floor rags and the spaces under a table or chair. They eat anything that drops to the floor and sustain their first major injury to their fingers or knees when a dog or an old person is watching. At the doctor's office, boys like that try to kiss everything but nobody thinks it's cute.

•

For the first five years of their lives, boys like that dress like girls. They wear shiny blouses with puffed sleeves and skirts with gold borders that sit prettily on their feet. Strings of jasmine hang across their heads, attracting small bees that only the boys can see. Thick smears of kajal make them look bewildered even though they have already understood the ant, the streaming of sunlight, and the technology of anger as contained in the heel and hand. Boys like that are given cricket bats and small rubber balls by visitors who wonder why they haven't got them already. Boys like that hold these things indifferently, forgetting them under chairs or beside trees. Boys like that don't speak for a long time because no one speaks to them. When they say their first word, they say it under their breath so no one can hear it. They do this on purpose.

•

Boys like that have one aunt or uncle who dies at thirty. They meet when the aunt/uncle is already dying from something that makes their breath smell like kerosene. This could be due to drug addiction, diseases of the blood or liver, excessive spirituality, tuberculosis, boredom, multiple attacks of typhoid or unrequited love. The aunt/uncle plays pranks that leave lifelong scars on the arms of boys like that. They show them pictures of men holding their penises like it is a heavy secret and women pinching nipples that look dry and tired. The aunt/uncle takes boys like that for walks in unsafe places and makes them read long before they are ready. During summer vacations, boys like that read about God, breasts, coming down from LSD, the sexual molestation of twelve-year-old white girls, Kashmiri pot, Kamala Das, the Tandoori murders, autism, bisexuality, cowboys, Americans eating, Americans praying, Americans fucking, Americans shooting people, people shooting Americans, English breakfasts, ghosts, computers and demons. Boys like that become fluent in English in the wrong way, so that people treat them either with suspicion or as wayward Christians. When the aunt/uncle finally dies, boys like that don't go for the funeral.

•

Boys like that leave spaces in other people's memories of cricket or watching blue films, spaces that are boy-shaped and difficult to fill.

Meanwhile, boys like that remember standing in front of packed chicken cages at the back of butcher shops. They remember how the chicken's wings opened uselessly when they were pulled out of the cage. They remember putting out their arms and screeching along with the chickens. Boys like that think of how death was a slice of afternoon wedged between the cage and the stump of wood cradling the thick, dirty knife, punctuated with cries that were clear and easy to understand, *please don't kill me like this, please don't kill me in this way, please don't, okay then goodbye everything and everyone, this hurts, this hurts so much and I don't want it to be happening but it is, okay then goodbye.* Boys like that don't become vegetarians.

•

Boys like that kiss boys before they kiss girls because that's just how it happens. They kiss bravely, like they are drinking water. They kiss and taste raw onions, the fuzz of an unbrushed mouth that just likes to eat toothpaste, the metallic tang of nervousness. Boys like that fall in love with the peeling of green paint in a splatter of light, with sleeping street dogs, with teachers, little sisters, with clouds, with bread and jam. Boys like that kiss for reasons they can never explain and no one ever understands.

•

Boys like that walk home slowly. They stay in rented rooms above biriyani stalls and hang their shirts on nails in the wall. They have tea and Marie biscuits for breakfast but they aren't friends with the tea stall owner. They have fathers who carry oily plastic bags and are always away doing business. These fathers appear suddenly, unshaven, smelling like rotten mangoes and young girls' hair. They eat ravenously, sleep on the floor and show people the wounds on their legs that refuse to heal. In the evenings, they cry pungent tears into the shoulders of boys like that and say that their legs are haunted by malignant spirits that are trying to eat them from the inside. The spirits have voices like KR Vijaya and are always hungry. Sometimes, the spirits appear as young girls with three breasts and force the fathers to have sex.

Boys like that give their fathers fifty rupees and their fathers make plans to stay—they say they will get milk in the morning so they can make tea at home. They make plans to buy their sons gas stoves and insurance policies. They ask why boys like that aren't married and don't have government jobs. Boys like that ask if it is true that they only had an eighteen percent chance of survival and the fathers say they will talk all about it tomorrow.

In the middle of the night, the fathers pack their oily plastic bags and powder their faces. They leave quickly, taking a shirt from the wall at the last minute. Boys like that watch them go.

saint diesel

The dragon is curled into the corner of an old cardboard box. His head is flat but lumpy with jagged edges. We have wrapped three layers of duct tape around his mouth because we are smart. The dragon looks at us with cloudy eyes and we feel sorry for him. "Everything is going to be alright," we say. We name him Saint Diesel, which is the perfect name for a dragon. We wait for him to sit up and stretch his wings so we can take pictures and post them on Facebook.

•

We buy chicken puffs, the nice ones, and wash our hands with Lifebuoy before we shred them. We pick out the onions—"No harm in being careful," says R. We place the shredded pieces around the dragon's snout and carefully remove the duct tape but he doesn't eat anything. We decide he isn't hungry and tape his mouth shut again. We try giving him milk and water but he doesn't drink anything either.

•

We take him to the balcony for an hour a day. R looks for a gentle spot of sunlight and I place the dragon in it with both hands. We watch dappled shadows slither across his body and wait for him to do something. His cloudy eyes stare at the sky while we point at his stomach and say he has definitely gained weight. R says, "Hey Diesel Diesel!" and whistles. Sometimes we think he recognizes us. Sometimes we decide he is just tired and take him back inside.

•

The dragon wails in the night. We lie awake, marvelling that he can wail so loud when his mouth is taped shut. We decide that he must be wailing through his nose, and that this must be something dragons can do which most people don't know about. We keep the dragon in the kitchen cupboard behind the rice bin but we can still hear him. R starts having anxiety dreams and indigestion. He calls the dragon a little shit but later he says he's sorry and he didn't mean it.

•

We leave the dragon in the kitchen cabinet to teach him a lesson. We spend the day on the balcony, watching the gentle spots of sunlight move across the spider webs and drifts of dust. R talks about his band in college and how they did an Indian version of the song "I'm in Love with Margaret Thatcher", but with Indira Gandhi. He cradles the ragged bits of sunlight in his hands and explains that the song was creative but you wouldn't get it if you weren't into punk. That evening, we check on the dragon. We look at his faded claws and run our fingers across the duct tape on his mouth. We decide he hasn't learned his lesson.

•

We realize we haven't checked on the dragon in three days. Tiny red ants have swarmed over the old pieces of chicken and some of them have climbed onto the dragon's arm. We decide they are too small to be harmful. The dragon's wings have turned grey and the edges have begun to fray. R removes the duct tape and a smell like old milk curls into the air. The smell clings to everything and makes us nauseous. We decide to let the dragon go tomorrow so that he can live under a tree or next to some flowering plants and be happy. We believe he will make friends, find natural sources of food and live for many years.

•

The day before we move, we find the empty cardboard box behind the rice bin. It smells like old milk. We decide that the dragon flew away on his own and is doing really well. We throw the box away but the smell sticks to our fingers and hair and doesn't go away for a long time.

kisi shayar
something something

Women's hostels always smell like limestone. Everyone gets tetanus from the rusty metal beds but we are used to the tetanus. It's the typhoidjaundicemalaria that brings us down. The bathrooms are overrun with sleek, black canals and boats slice through them like angry fish. Sailors stand on the decks and tell us to take our tops off. Some girls throw chunks of soap at them. Others faint and we have to fish them out of the water. Sometimes we let them drown.

My bed is at the end of the hall. The girl beside me is stacking notebooks on her writing table and singing an old Hindi song.

Dream Girl, kisi shayar...

She frowns. And then she fills in the missing words with something something.

Kisi shayar something something, Dream Girl

"Have you seen the bathrooms yet?" I ask.

"Why, are there cameras? Did you find the cameras?" says the girl. The bathrooms usually have hidden cameras. We can't see them because they are the size of dimes and we don't know what a dime looks like. We do know that the cameras are sprinkled all over the walls and doors. We know that the footage is sold to sheiks in Dubai. She shrugs and starts wrapping her books with brown paper.

"I'm not bothered," she says. "I will bathe with a towel on."

She is one of those pros who can wrap a book without using glue or rice to hold the paper down. Everything is sharp and straight and as it should be. There is a sudden, muffled splash as another girl falls into a canal.

"There should be a fence," I say. "Nobody would fall in if there was a fence."

"They would just climb the fence and fall in anyway," says the girl. "That's the kind of hostel this is. You know what I mean?"

She opens her suitcase and pulls out a metal plate and a metal tumbler.

"Anyway," she says, "I'm off for dinner."

She locks her suitcase with a key that she wears on a string around her neck. A group of girls are waiting for her, each one carrying a metal plate and a metal tumbler, each one wearing her suitcase key on a string around her neck. They wade carefully through the flooded corridor while the hair of drowning girls clings to their ankles.

I will strew slum roads with 25 paisa coins
and feel like a freedom fighter.

I will hide 50 paisa coins under rocks as a special surprise
for poor people who look under rocks.

you can't
and you don't

People like to take pictures of him eating. He wears a baseball cap and holds his knife and fork like he is ready for anything. Everyone is touched that he still eats this way. In the pictures, he is usually staring down at plates piled with chicken, his mouth slightly open. "Eats and fucks anything that walks" they say. And then they laugh like he is laughing with them.

He is spotted in bars that were popular in the seventies and have waiters who look like they never go home. He is usually with four or five other men who are referred to as The Malaysian Mafia. He has two cell phones and everyone thinks this is suspicious. They say he is trying to be a movie star or a politician but can't decide which is worse.

Girls who thought he was adorable have become women who think he is chee. They don't feel comfortable inviting him for anything unless there are other men around. They say he is a sideychick magnet. Young girls with long, shiny legs make him promise to drop them home because they will be so scared to take an auto alone in the night dressed like this because what if something happens? These girls look slum but they wear miniskirts and speak English and everyone thinks this is disturbing.

People suggest he is balding and everyone says yes, this is why he wears the baseball caps. Someone thinks he should just shave his head because young bald men are sexy. He isn't young anymore, says one of the women. Everyone agrees that baseball caps will make the balding worse.

They remember when he used to help push buses that had broken down in the middle of the road. If there had been an accident, he would direct traffic until a policeman would tell him to get lost. They remember how he made friendship bracelets and tied them around people's wrists when they weren't looking.

this old man

The sun was dripping from the window, popping against the floor like tiny bubbles of electricity. The old man heard laughter and thought of people standing outside in the dust, baring their mouths to the sky. They are laughing, he said to himself and yet he kept thinking of yellow lines of teeth stretching into the horizon like tombstones.

The old man sighed and opened his eyes. He saw the old plastic bucket in front of him, half-filled with clear, yellowish water. A faded blue rag was neatly folded on the floor beside his feet. There was also a red plastic dustpan. He frowned, trying to remember what it was for.

"Dustpan?" he said.

His daughter was sitting at the far end of the room with her back to him. She no longer turned when she spoke to him. The old man couldn't remember why but he was sure she had a good reason.

"What?" she said.

"The dustpan. What's it for?"

She didn't answer or maybe she did and he didn't hear her.

"I'll just keep it to the side then," he said. "I don't think I will need it."

"Do what you want, Appa."

He could hear the women in the kitchen downstairs, rustling like dry leaves inside their saris. The first time he heard them he was reminded of half-formed butterflies shuffling and turning inside their cocoons. A little while later, his mouth had overflowed with blue and silver caterpillars, each one carrying a stunted wing on its back. The old man tried to count them as they drowned in the bucket but he couldn't remember what came after the number 5. Another time it had been feathers. They had crashed into the back of his teeth and hung from his lips and chin like a clumsy beard. He couldn't remember what he was thinking about when the feathers happened. The old man heard the women speak about children who had died in the womb, how the weather turned when one least expected it. There was the popping of oil on the stove, the smell of melting sugar. And then it was time.

He caught the sides of the bucket to steady himself. Then with a loud retch, the old man heaved, his entire body shuddering as if it was about to break. When it was over, silver strings of saliva dripped from his lips as he caught his breath. In the bucket he saw a Christmas card, a broken comb, his old blue fountain pen. Fragments of words and forgotten diseases bobbed like dead fish in a pool of vomit and yellow water. He pulled shredded photographs and snippets of his wife's hair from between his teeth.

"I'm sorry I can't help, Appa," said his daughter. "It's the puke smell—I'm sorry."

The old man shook his head. She didn't have to do anything. He was fine. He stared down at the pieces of his life and marvelled at how small and insignificant everything was.

"What good is a woman if she can't even clean up a man's vomit?" his daughter said. "What's the good of that Appa?"

Once at a bus stand, the old man had watched a woman pick up a piece of dirty string and tie it around her wrist. He had felt something squirm at the roof of his mouth, like a strand of hair. That was when it started, he thought to himself, although he knew it wasn't true.

The smell of hot oil and sugar draped itself in a thick curtain along the room. He felt the nausea start like a whisper in the pit of his throat. It blossomed slowly, reminding him of women who tied strings around their wrists.

"What are they making downstairs? I keep forgetting," said the old man.

"It's Deepavali Appa. They're making sweets."

"It can't be. It's too early for Deepavali."

"Then it's Pongal. It's Onam. Christmas. Bakrid. Independence Day. It's everybody's birthday."

"Can you turn on the fan? The smell is making me nauseous."

"But it's Deepavali 'Pa."

It's not Deepavali, the old man thought to himself. He felt like saying it out loud, just to see what would happen. Say it. Say It's Not Deepavali. It's Not Anything. But the old man's mouth would only hang open like an empty bag. On second thought, don't say anything at all, he said to himself. Close your mouth. Don't say anything.

He heard the rustle of silk as a woman gently glided up the stairs. Sometimes it was his sister-in-law. Sometimes it was his wife. Sometimes it was just a woman.

"Have some," said the woman, thrusting a plate of sweets under his nose. It was filled with bright orange jalebis, each one glowing like a syrupy burning wire.

"Eat," she said. "There is more, I will bring you."

"No, please," said the old man. "I can't—"

"Don't worry, there's more," said the woman.

"I really can't. But if someone could bring me a lime. Or a piece of ginger…"

"I'll bring more," said the woman. "There's lots more."

She glided down the stairs and the old man heard the sizzle of things being dipped and atrophied in hot oil.

"Can't you ask them to stop?" said the old man to his daughter. "If they just stopped for a while—"

"It's Deepavali, 'Pa. You can't ask them to stop making sweets on Deepavali."

When he was a boy, the old man had watched his mother burn herself while frying murukku. Her skin had bubbled and blistered and he worried that it would spread to him if he touched her.

"Did I ever tell you—" said the old man.

"Yes," said his daughter.

"What?"

"Yes, you've told me what happened."

"About how my mother—"

"Yes, she was frying jamoons and she burnt her face off."

"No, she—"

"You've already told me 'Pa."

Downstairs, the women laughed and hissed along with the oil. He looked at the braid that hung down his daughter's back like a dead snake. He had a feeling that was all that was left of her. In a way, he was glad she didn't turn around anymore. The old man looked into the bucket and saw tattered bits of a family photograph, bumping halfheartedly against the sides.

"What happened to your sister?" asked the old man.

"What do you mean?"

"Why doesn't she call anymore? Why doesn't she come and see me?"

"Why would she do that?"

"It's Deepavali, isn't it? Why doesn't she come and see me? Why doesn't anyone come and see me?"

She didn't answer or maybe she did and he didn't hear her. The old man sighed and closed his eyes. He heard dry strands of laughter hovering outside in the heat. They are laughing, he thought to himself. It's Deepavali and they are laughing. All the children are wrapped in dirty pieces of string. In the night they will watch the firecrackers bubble and blister into their skin. Everybody is laughing.

The old man heard the sun drip from the window, popping against the floor like tiny bubbles of electricity. He opened his eyes and saw the old plastic bucket in front of him, half-filled with clear, yellowish water. A faded blue rag lay neatly folded on the floor beside his feet. There was also a red plastic dustpan.

He frowned, trying to remember what it was for.

discuss how india
will become a
prosperous and secure nation
in the next five years

I will brush my teeth twice a day. I will activate the circulation in my gums using a swift up and down motion that will cause my gums to bleed like the sun leaking through a heavy sky. I will spit thin strips of blood into the sink and feel marvellous and vital. I will speak to old people who are curved and dying, inhaling the rot of their ripe mouths while I press my tongue against the strong lines of my teeth. I will smile at them even if they don't smile at me.

•

I will drop spare change on the ground for poor people to find. I will strew slum roads with 25 paisa coins and feel like a freedom fighter. I will hide 50 paisa coins under rocks as a special surprise for poor people who look under rocks. I will smile benevolently at suicidal farmers and encourage them to name their tractors after me. I will lift their children into the air with both hands, holding them against the sky so the sun doesn't get in my eyes. I will say "Jai Hind" so that everyone will have to say "Jai Hind" after me.

•

I will see Mother Mary in mysorepaks that are stacked and cobwebbed in dilapidated sweet stalls. I will think of the missionary story about bread and how Jesus likes brown people best: "Yellow bread is mouldy. White bread is uncooked. Black bread is burnt. But brown bread is perfect." I will think of how Jesus likes brown bread because we are perfect. When people close their eyes and start talking about the best mysorepaks they have ever eaten, I will tell them I've had an intense spiritual experience but I can't talk about it because they wouldn't understand.

Under a broken cot at the back of the house lives an albino killer whale that sings "Ireland Must Be Heaven, For My Mother Came From There" through its blowhole. During the night and on very hot afternoons, the whale hurls itself into the sky like it wants to die.

daily future life predictions
from the
hotmalluauntywetsarisexboobs
dotcomcenter
based in the
tropicool icy-land
urban indian slum

Monday

Today you will find money in the pocket of your new blue shirt. One of the bills will have *I Love You LilyMalar 420* written on the back and even though your name is not LilyMalar you will blush. You will feel apprehensive because you are sure this money is not yours. In order to feel safer, you will close the only window in your room. Leafy sea dragons will cluster on your windowsill to see what you are hiding. They will say *who's the small loser* when you knock them off the windowsill with a broken pencil. They will leave behind streaks of algae on purpose. In the evening you will think of the streaks on your windowsill and feel lonely. You will <u>click here</u> because you know I take off all my clothes and put everything in my mouth for you.

Tuesday

Today you will wear the blue shirt again because you found money in it yesterday and you think the same thing will happen today. Today you will find dead seahorses in the pocket. The leafy sea dragons will cluster on your windowsill to see what you are hiding and you will feel guilty about the dead seahorses and the money, though neither is your fault. You will throw all your ration kerosene on the leafy sea dragons and they will say *who's the small loser* before dying on your windowsill. You will collect all the dead bodies in a yellow cloth bag and throw them in an abandoned municipal garbage bin. You will see a gang of Gentoo penguins pass by and you will be convinced that they saw you kill the leafy sea dragons. Overcome with guilt, you will go home and <u>click here</u> because I love it when you cum in my mouth baby.

Wednesday

Today you will throw the blue shirt in the abandoned municipal garbage bin because you think it is unlucky. People will ask why you keep throwing things in abandoned garbage bins. Someone will say they saw you throw something in there yesterday and someone else will say I saw you too, it looked just like you and you will say "I don't know him!" and they will say "Him what him?" You will spend the afternoon at home, watching an albino killer whale hurl itself into the sky. You will promise yourself that tomorrow you will act like nothing happened and you will be normal. As a reward for being normal tomorrow, you will <u>click here</u> today to see me fully without dress ready to make big hot sexy for you.

Thursday

You will stay inside all morning. You will look at the streaks of algae on the windowsill and forget about the money. Then you will remember the money and you will go out and blow it all on three large cases of Minty-Fresh Export-Quality Aadi Velli Special Non-Cola Cola. This will make you feel angry and stupid. In your anger, you will corner a lone Gentoo penguin and ask it what it knows. Then you will tell the penguin that it knows nothing. The Gentoo penguin will call you a sanitary napkin sucker and you will beat the penguin to death with sloppy fists and throw its body in the abandoned municipal garbage bin. Later, you will click here to see me but I won't be there. Instead, you will see my friend who is a city college girl doing bending exercise in bra and fanty.

Friday

You will have nightmares that a gang of Gentoo penguins keeps jumping on your face while the albino killer whale hurls itself up and down, up and down without helping you. After waking up you will feel scared. Then you will feel proactive and scrub the algae streaks off your windowsill. You will drink three bottles of Non-Cola Cola and vomit continuously for the next hour. In the night, you will stand at the window and wish you hadn't thrown away the blue shirt because you really liked it. You will also think you are a murderer and sometimes a pervert. You will not <u>click here</u> to see my naughty servant girl giving me full body oil massage. Instead, you will fall asleep and dream that I am taking off your shirt and spitting hot kerosene in your face.

Saturday

After the bodies of the leafy sea dragons, the seahorses and the Gentoo penguin are found in the abandoned garbage bin, the slum will be under curfew in anticipation of communal violence. Your blue shirt will be recovered and three policemen will bring it to your door. You will give them the rest of your Non-Cola Cola and they will give you the shirt and leave. You will set the sleeve of the shirt on fire and throw it out the window. It will land on the man who sells Non-Cola Colas and you will watch his hair and shoulders catch fire. You will decide to buy a new blue shirt tomorrow. Then you will <u>click here</u> to have sweetsexy Saturday chat with me because I love you long time and Sunday is my holiday.

transcripts from interviews
with
three spiritual entities
trapped inside a young girl
in the
tropicool icy-land
urban indian slum

SPIRITUAL ENTITY 1

I remember when we first came here there was this huge traffic jam in front of that Ambedkar Primary whatever, that school? It's a school, right? Yeah, and we thought it was the kids that were blocking the road but when we got closer, we saw it was this huge whale. And it was just lying there in the middle of the road, like drying out and stuff and no one was putting water on it or anything, they were just climbing over it and doing whatever. And someone said it was drunk—the *whale* was *drunk*—and it always did this when it was drunk and I didn't really understand that but I was like okay different cultures and everything. But it was really weird for me because I had never seen anything like that before. And later we saw these penguins stealing a bicycle and that was really weird for me too. I guess all of that should have clued us in a bit though.

SPIRITUAL ENTITY 2

There's definitely a feeling of disappointment because I know we were all in this to win. Mistakes have been made; I think there's been a lot of discussion about whether we should have come to the Tropicool Icy-Land in the first place. This was just a very, very tough project. But it's important to remember that we fought hard and put in our best effort. Now we're just feeling really excited and positive about getting out and moving on. We're very excited about that.

SPIRITUAL ENTITY 3

Have you ever seen a whale? Like actually seen one up close? Those are big motherfuckers. And they can explode, like after they die and if they're on land, they will decompose so much they explode and there's like blubber hanging from the trees and it smells really really bad. This whale was just drunk so there was no risk of it blowing up or anything. I was thinking it probably takes a lot of alcohol to get a whale drunk. Like a *lot*.

•

SPIRITUAL ENTITY 1

There used to be fifteen of us. Sometimes we would just hang out, you know, play I Spy or something. And that was fun. But when it came to the girl, we couldn't get it together, it just never worked, you know? Like I remember this one time we finally had her slithering up the wall like a snake and then this electric eel shows up and was like "Hey what-tha fuck-ya? What-tha fuck?" Because apparently they get really touchy if people start acting like electric eels here because it's like racist or something. And I didn't really get that because it was an eel and I didn't get how eels were racist but apparently this slum has a lot of communal issues and things would have really gotten out of hand for us if we had kept that up so—

And the funny thing was that it wasn't even an electric eel, it was a snake, so obvious if you looked at the body movement. Anyway.

SPIRITUAL ENTITY 2

This venture definitely had some unique challenges. None of us expected that it would be so difficult to get things moving; we couldn't accomplish anything at all, despite our best efforts. We definitely underestimated the toll it would take on our team as well. As I've said before, very, very tough project. But we've learned so much. We're ready to put this behind us now but we've learned so, so much.

SPIRITUAL ENTITY 3

Then I was thinking, well how does it get the alcohol down? Something that size is probably taking the bottles along with the alcohol, right? So there must be an awful lot of bottles inside that whale. And I was thinking, are they shored up against the ribs or does it shit them out or do they dissolve inside the body or something? And I remembered that whales have fluorescent shit. So there's the fluorescent shit and at least a million liquor bottles in there. I really wanted to go in and see but nobody would come with me and there's no way I'm going out there alone. It's the whales that have the fluorescent shit, right?

•

Spiritual Entity 1

I think we should have paid more attention to the cultural thing. Because in India, they're really into abusing women, like they don't let them wear pants or learn English and stuff. So why would they bother about a girl who's got fifteen demons in her? And now there's just three of us left and they're still like, yeah? So? I mean why would they bother with an exorcism if they won't even let this girl go to school so she can learn how to wear pants and get a job? Bottom line, nobody here cares about spirit possession when it happens to a girl. She had fifteen of us in her, *fifteen!* And nobody cared. And it's not like they don't have exorcisms here. They do them all the time, for men, I'm guessing. Or rich women, probably. There is a real exorcist right here in this slum. Her name is JoMol and she lives just down the road there, she has a biriyani stall. You can't miss her, wears a red nightdress, black glasses. She does them all the time, two hours tops, you should call her. I'm serious, call her. Because no one here will. No one cares. I think you could really make a difference if you called JoMol and made her exorcise us. You could really change this girl's life and make it better and give her a future.

Spiritual Entity 2

I have tremendous, tremendous professional respect for JoMol. And I think because of that great respect we would be more than happy to oblige her. If she thinks it's time for us to leave, I say great! Let's do it! I believe it's time for us to move on anyway, it's important to try new things and not get tied down to one place for too long.

She lives down the road, just down there. I can show you from the window. Come here, I'll show you.

Spiritual Entity 3

It's a little complicated because there's just three of us now but the others are still in here. They're kind of dead or something but they're still in here. This has never happened to me before so I don't really know but I'm thinking it's not good to have dead spirits in here like this. And the girl is going on like normal and everyone else is going on like normal and no one seems bothered about any of this except us. And I can't help thinking that we should have gotten into the whale instead, you know? Because it was just drunk, it wasn't dead. And if you can possess dogs and horses then why not whales? And when I suggested it back then, everyone was like no, it's in the water, what can you do in the water. And I was like, are you fucking kidding me? Leviathan, hello! Attack of the Giant Squid, hello! Rabid, possessed whale eats Greenpeace ships—you can see that, right? That could totally happen. It could still happen. I mean if you could get us out of here and maybe find the whale again. Or if you could just get us out of here, that would be great. That would really help us out a lot.

three scenarios
leading to
the rape of a teenage girl
in the
tropicool icy-land
urban indian slum

I.

Girl is between the ages of 13 and 18. Father has committed suicide, mother cooks idlies for a living, and the younger brother works in a factory making things with lead and mercury. The family bicycle is stolen every night by a gang of Gentoo penguins. Overwhelmed with remorse, the penguins return the bicycle each morning with a note of apology which flies away before anyone can see it.

The girl is named Lakshmi. She has long, thick hair and a patch of leucoderma on her right shoulder which people often mistake for leprosy. Lakshmi takes care of rich people's children and dreams of paying off her family's debts. She does not dream of ice cream though she once dreamed of a frozen waterfall which looked like a giant blue curtain.

Lakshmi goes out late at night to buy milk. Suddenly, it starts raining and she takes shelter in a liquor store plastered with posters of women straddling giant vodka bottles. A bicycle slowly teeters past with guilt-ridden penguins clinging to the seat and handlebars.

2.

Girl is between the ages of 13 and 18. Father is an alcoholic, mother makes sari blouses for a living, and the twin brother has run away to Mumbai to become a stunt double in the movies. Under a broken cot at the back of the house lives an albino killer whale that sings "Ireland Must Be Heaven, For My Mother Came From There" through its blowhole. During the night and on very hot afternoons, the whale hurls itself into the sky like it wants to die.

The girl is named Selvi. She has large breasts and her teeth are stained a deep brown due to dental flourosis. Selvi works in a fabric store and dances while doing mundane tasks. She dreams of buying her mother a new sewing machine. She does not dream of men though she does dream of disembodied moustaches that crawl up her leg.

Selvi walks home late at night. Suddenly, it starts raining and she turns into a dark sidestreet, looking for a rickshaw. The albino killer whale arches above her head like a curl of silver, singing "For her eyes are like the starlight, and the white clouds match her hair."

3.

Girl is between the ages of 13 and 18 with the mental development of a girl of 6. She has no mother, father is a retired school teacher with tuberculosis and the blind older brother sells mousepads for a living. The kitchen is haunted by a walrus that writes threatening notes to the family, claiming it will explode and cause decomposing blubber to rain on them while they are sleeping. These threats are written on the wall with charcoal and are wiped away each time the walrus moves around the cramped kitchen.

The girl is named Malli. She has a voluptuous figure and almond-shaped eyes. Every evening after dinner, Malli sings for her father and brother. This warms their hearts and fills them with mournful thoughts of how wonderful their life would have been if Malli was normal. She does not dream of anything.

Malli goes out late at night to catch a kitten she has seen on the road. Suddenly, it starts raining. The kitten disappears into an abandoned building and Malli follows it.

Elsewhere, the walrus writes "Chubby Rain, Motherfuckers" in cursive letters and carefully steps away from the wall.

the importance of having
a minty-fresh export-quality
aadi velli special non-cola cola
in the tropicool icy-land
urban indian slum

Just you taste and tell. I don't want you to buy it also madam. Simply you have it. Because you can be thinking, who is this loose fellow giving away this cool drinks on such a hot day like it is his father-in-law's property? Is he a crack? I tell you frankly madam. Money will come and go. If we cannot have some basic helping nature for fellow man, then what is there?

Just let me tell you. Other day one tourist fellow came, so very much upset. He said my cycle is stolen where is police station my cycle is stolen. I said okay, you just sit and tell what happened and you be free. All are your friends only. He said I don't want your friends bloodynonsense. Fully fuckfuck language he was saying—please don't mistake me madam—fully fuckfuck language he was saying also because some blackguard had absconded with his moneypurse and our Indian foods are making him very much upset. Then last night means he saw outside some penguins are stealing his cycle. He said at international level so many places I have travelled. Never in my life like this has occurred. Is it so common in India? I said stealing is common in so many countries. He said why penguins are stealing cycles? Is it a correct way for penguins to behave? I said why for you? Why you want to roam around on cycle thinking this is Goa or Switzerland? India has so many wonderful things like Taj Mahal and many temples. Also many churches and mosques because all religions like one are together here. Why you want to come all the way simply to cycle round and round in mofussil slum area?

Then I gave him this one tumbler, I said you just relax, have this, taste and see. I don't want you to buy also. Simply you have it. He said Indian cool drinks are making him take vomit. I said you please don't afraid. This is not your American PepsiCocaCola. This is hundred years Indian tradition AyurvedaHomoeopathySiddhaUnani medicine herbs for lowering heat, cholesterol, blood pressure, mental depression, piles, kidney stones, paralysis and marriage failure. Just you taste and see. If you fall sick I myself will take you to hospital. So he had. Then I called one auto, said take this fellow to bus stand, gave some money from my own pocket also. He said so many days I have been in your country only now God is showing me a true friend. I said all Indians are true friends. Except the thirutturascals who stole your cycle and moneypurse all Indians are true friends only. He said nono, *penguins* stole my cycle. I said okok you go see Taj Mahal and enjoy.

Why I am saying means, what can we do? If we have two hands and legs means we should also help our fellow man. If you can do so, give him some cool drinks, let him be free. If you can do nothing then you leave it. So only I am saying to you, just you relax, taste and tell madam. I don't want you to buy at all. Just you have it. If afterwards means you really want, bottle is just 375 rupees, bottle return.

a basic guide to
instigating violence
among gentoo penguins
in the
tropicool icy-land
urban indian slum

GENERAL GUIDELINES

1. Do not instigate violence if the Minty-Fresh Export-Quality Aadi Velli Special Non-Cola Cola stall is closed.

2. Though it is a well-documented fact that Gentoo penguins like to steal bicycles, this must never be mentioned as it will tap into a large pool of communal guilt which will cause the penguins to commit a very elaborate form of mass suicide.

3. Avoid problems later. Invest in quality loudspeakers and other products to save time and money.

4. Be Indian. Buy Indian.

THE ACTIVIST METHOD

1. Convince a group of Gentoo penguins that it is your birthday and you want to treat them to some Minty-Fresh Export-Quality Aadi Velli Special Non-Cola Cola to celebrate. Agree to meet them outside a centrally located Non-Cola Cola stall and insist on no gifts though you will accept charitable donations made in your name. Dress in loose-fitting cotton clothes and fill your pockets with dead seahorses. Carry a loudspeaker.

2. Smile benevolently when the assembled penguins sing "Happy Birthday" and present you with a bicycle lock as a gift. Accept both the song and the gift very graciously. Compliment the assembled penguins on their appearance and tell them that chilled bottles of Non-Cola Cola are shining and waiting for them like frosted unicorns.

3. The penguins will become mesmerized by the phrase "frosted uni-corns" in three phases. First, they will think you are talking about a goods train that travels across Russia. Then they will think you are talking about that white horse in *The Lord of the Rings*. Finally, they will realize you are talking about Non-Cola Cola bottles that shine like unicorns blinged out with frost. Once their eyes widen in wonder, turn on your loudspeaker and say "Who enslaved humans of colour? Who invaded the Caribbean? Who murdered all the innocent children? You did! You! You!"

4. The Gentoo penguins will be confused and angry that you have accused them of slavery and invading the Caribbean. This will cause their eyes to flush and shudder as images of blinged out unicorns, the white horse from *The Lord of the Rings* and a goods train slicing like a knife through Russia quickly flash before their eyes. Take advantage of this opportu-nity to hurl the dead seahorses at the penguins with great velocity. If possible, throw many handfuls of seahorses using a Windmills of Death motion. Simultaneously scream the words "anarchist," "blood rain," and "Pol Pot."

5. At this point, the Gentoo penguins will be gripped by rage and a growing horror that dead seahorses are falling from the sky. Use the loud-speaker to say "U-G-L-Y You Ain't Got No Alibi You Ugly Hey Hey You Ugly." Repeat the phrase "You Ugly" while sloppily thrusting your pelvis back and forth. The penguins will begin to scream, thus signalling the beginning of great violence.

THE MEIN HERR METHOD

1. Tell the Gentoo penguins that you are really sorry for the previous Violent Cola and Dead Seahorses Incident and you want to treat them to some Minty-Fresh Export-Quality Aadi Velli Special Non-Cola Cola to show how genuinely sorry you are. Say that you will bring the Non-Cola Cola to them because it's the least you can do. Dress in a casual state of mourning and carry dead seahorses in both pockets. Bring a loudspeaker.

2. Smile benevolently when the penguins assemble in silence and look at you under hooded eyes that are crisscrossed and starred with suspicion. Start to cry and say "I wish I hadn't done that stupid stupid Violent Cola and Dead Seahorses Thing because it was just so stupid and it was just the stupidest thing ever and I am so stupid." It may be necessary to repeat this two to three times. At some point, the Gentoo penguins will assure you that you aren't stupid. Smile and compliment the assembled penguins on their appearance and tell them that chilled bottles of Non-Cola Cola are shining and waiting for them like frosted unicorns.

3. Once the penguins become mesmerized by the phrase "frosted unicorns," bring out the bottles one by one so that the cancerous slum sunlight ricochets off the iced bottles like crushed lightning. As soon as each penguin has a flipper outstretched in anticipation, smash every single bottle to the ground. Turn on your loudspeaker and say "Bye bye mein lieber Herr, auf wiedersehen, mein Herr, es war sehr gut, mein Herr, und vorbei, du kennst mich wohl, mein Herr, ach, lebe wohl, mein Herr, du sollst mich nie mehr sehen mein Herr." Then run away very quickly.

4. The Gentoo penguins will be confused and angry that you have not only broken the bottles and run away, but you may have also called them bad words in a foreign language. Climb onto the balcony of a nearby building and shout "It's German, you stupid penguins. Don't you know German? Don't you know Liza Minnelli in Cabaret? Don't you know anything, you stupid penguins?" Begin hurling the dead seahorses at the penguins with great velocity. If possible, throw the seahorses like Ninja Stars of Death. Simultaneously scream the words "mentalist," "genetically modified eggplants," and "Manchurian Candidate."

5. At this point, the Gentoo penguins will be gripped by rage and a sense that this same sequence of events has happened to them before. Use the loudspeaker to say "U-G-L-Y You Ain't Got No Alibi You Ugly Hey Hey You Ugly." Repeat the phrase "You Ugly" while holding a walrus in front of you and sloppily thrusting your pelvis back and forth. The penguins will begin to scream, thus signalling the beginning of great violence.

THE RE-ACTIVIST METHOD

1. Tell the Gentoo penguins that you are really sorry about the previous two Violent Cola and Dead Seahorses Incidents and you want to treat them to some Minty-Fresh Export-Quality Aadi Velli Special Non-Cola Cola to show how genuinely sorry you are. Say that you will bring the Non-Cola Cola along with glossy magazines filled with lots of boobies. Wear a t-shirt that says "Gentoo Penguins Did Not Steal Your Bicycle Dumbass". Carry dead seahorses in a fanny pack. Bring a loudspeaker.

2. Bow your head with contrition when the penguins tell you to go fuck yourself and make an obscene gesture in a swift, choreographed motion. Start to cry. When the Gentoo penguins tell you to stop crying, cry louder. Climb onto a nearby roof and say "I wish I hadn't done that stupid stupid Violent Cola and Dead Seahorses Thing because I already did it once and then I did it again and it was just so stupid and I am so stupid and now I am going to kill myself." Waver dangerously at the edge. The assembled penguins will form a Penguin Catchment Area beneath you and say you are not stupid and you should not jump because you are young and you should live. Smile and compliment the assembled penguins on their appearance and tell them that chilled bottles of Non-Cola Cola are shining and waiting for them like frosted unicorns.

3. As the penguins become mesmerized by the phrase "frosted unicorns," quickly break out the Non-Cola Cola and pour it into fancy glasses. Juggle a few bottles and flip ice cubes off your arm into the glasses. Ask the penguins in the front if they are having a good time and who's from farthest away. Then ask if they want to see something special but do not wait for an answer. Pour all the Non-Cola Cola into a bucket and say Ready? When they say Ready! throw the bucket and the Non-Cola Cola at the penguins. Turn on your loudspeaker and say "Promote ideology! Fascism! Promote individual interests! George Stephanopoulos! Imelda Marcos! Sugar! Beef! Bananas! Pork bellies! Lumber! Coca-Cola! The information superhighway!"

4. The Gentoo penguins will be confused and angry that they have been molested with Non-Cola Cola and also because they will not know and will not like the names George Stephanopoulos and Imelda Marcos. Begin hurling dead seahorses at the penguins with great velocity. If possible, throw the seahorses in a Windmill Ninja Stars of Death motion. Simultaneously scream the words "xenophobia," "environmental terrorism," and "we're being attacked by Hottentots."

5. At this point, the Gentoo penguins will be gripped by rage heightened with humiliation as they realize this is something that has happened twice already and it is happening again. This will cause them to bristle with indignation, a physical state that Gentoo penguins cannot endure for long periods of time. At this point, use the loudspeaker to say "U-G-L-Y You Ain't Got No Alibi You Ugly Hey Hey You Ugly." Repeat the phrase "You Ugly" while you are sandwiched between a walrus and a sea lion, sloppily thrusting your pelvis back and forth. The penguins will try to smother their collective scream so they may focus on their bristling. This will cause them to simultaneously combust. Hot, angry pieces of penguin will block out the sun and rain upon the urban Indian slum in fat, lazy drops of ferocious blood and cartilage. Beaks and flippers will clog the gutters, causing sewage to overflow into the street and pipefish and leafy sea dragons to die in such numbers that an albino killer whale will start hurling itself into the sky screaming "Genocide Genocide Mother of God Oh the humanity Oh the horror horror!" thus signalling the beginning of great violence.

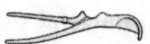

Hero and Heroine drink hot bottles of sambar
and sing an upbeat song about baby boys that are like suns
and hearts that turn into kites.

whore

I will meet you on a bus. I will be thinking of the Pulveli song from *Aasai* when you will come up from behind and put your hand on my hand. I will not realize what you are doing until your hand is on the side of my breast and you are whispering "sexy whore" into the back of my neck. I will turn suddenly and this will make people think I have dropped something. An old man will shuffle to the side and a boy with a backpack will point to a broken earring on the floor and say "there, there". You will have a scrubbed face, white teeth and clean hands. This will make me think it couldn't have been you. I will look for men who are dark and dirty with red eyes but I will be too shaken to see anything. It is only when you get off the bus and wave at me that I will realize it was you. At work, I will hear someone say that newspapers only report rape cases because of the sex appeal. Someone else will say that Delhi offers cash incentives for men to rape women. Everyone will laugh at this and I will laugh with them while the Pulveli song runs in a loop inside my head.

•

Every morning for one month, you will get on the bus to grind your hand into my waist or grab the back of my thigh. You will usually pinch the side of my breast and say "sexy whore". I will try to move to the front or to another bus. I will try to stab you with pins, geometry compasses and fountain pens. I will try to stamp your feet, scratch your hand or hit you in the groin but nothing will work. Each time it starts, I will tell myself it is just the edge of the seat, an aunty's handbag or my imagination. When I can no longer tell myself these things, I will stare out the window with the Pulveli song in my head and think that you are right, I must be a whore because I am letting this happen. Over the next month, I will develop ulcers and patches of eczema on my face and arms. I will stop wearing T-shirts, jeans, short-sleeved salwars, earrings and open-toed sandals, even though this will not make any difference. Friends will tell me that I have a vitamin deficiency and I should take better care of myself. I will take multi-vitamin supplements but that won't make any difference either.

•

I will dream of you. I will be walking in a crowded building with walls that keep swallowing small children. People will laugh and pull the children out while the Pulveli song plays in the background. You will be surrounded by young women who watch as you crack open a dusty cocoon and drag out a tiny, naked girl by the hair. They will clap when you dangle her above your mouth and sing "Jumma Chumma De De". I will try to call you a motherfucker, throw hot oil in your face and grind my heel into your blistering eyes. But all I will be able to do is clap along with them.

•

After a month, it will all be over. You will disappear and I will panic each time I see someone who looks like you. My face and arms will be peppered with scars from the eczema but my ulcer will heal. I will have the national anthem as my ringtone. I will like someone's Facebook post that says "most rapes would not happen if girls dressed and behaved with common sense, this is not the West". I will pin my dupatta to my kurta. I will stop talking to the men at work. I will not take the bus. I will tell myself that it is no big deal, that I'll forget all about it one day. Sometimes this will make me feel better.

the good place

We kept the angel in a glass bottle. It had tattered, leathery wings which hung forlornly from its shoulders. Its long, yellow nails perched against the glass while one dark blue eye looked at the lights, then us, then the lights again. Its other eye was sealed shut. Kavin wanted to keep the angel. He wanted to build it a shoebox-house, feed it whiskey, and take it to a church to see what would happen.

"It's not an angel," I said.

"It used to be," said Kavin.

"It isn't now," I said.

Kavin and I had never seen The Good Place but we knew it was somewhere in the atmosphere, hiding behind the acid rain. In the beginning, when it was still perfecting itself, it sloughed off debris, shaking off anything it didn't need and littering the ground with asbestos, child pornography, genetically modified foods and monosodium glutamate. The last thing it dumped was the angels. They could be found tangled in the tops of trees, diminished, atrophied, usually dead. It was rare to find one that was still alive.

"We could sell it," said Kavin, tapping at the glass. "How much do you think people would pay for an angel?"

"It's not an angel," I said.

"It's a vestigial angel," said Kavin. "Perfect for decorative purposes. Gifting purposes. Paperweight. EtceteraEtcetera."

He yawned and got up, making his way to the bathroom with slow, measured steps. I unscrewed the cap of the bottle and a puff of warm, oily air bloomed up, gently touching my cheeks and mouth.

"What does 'vestigial' mean?" asked the angel.

Its wings rustled gently, sending down a shower of dry, brown flakes that settled around its feet.

"Is it like vertigo?" asked the angel.

"No," I said.

"Then?"

"It's when something becomes useless because of the evolution of something."

"Okay," said the angel. "I think I get it."

Its wings rustled again and a muffled snap seemed to echo inside the bottle.

"Kavin's an asshole," I said. "I guess I'm an asshole too though."

"Angels don't have assholes," said the angel. "Most people don't know that."

I looked at the angel's crumpled shoulders, the mouldy skin hanging from its arms and stomach, its puckered, black mouth. At one time, it had probably been magnificent, creating rivers and thunderstorms by shaking its hair. It had probably carried clouds on its shoulders and looked like the sun. People would have named children, flowering plants, and tiny shimmering fish after it.

"Our tailbones are vestigial," I said. "But I guess it's not the same thing."

"When you all turn into tailbones it will be the same thing," said the angel.

I looked over at the bathroom door, hoping Kavin would suddenly appear, wiping his hands on his jeans.

"You should ask me something," said the angel.

"Like what?"

"Ask me anything. Ask me if you're really an asshole."

I picked up the cap of the bottle—we hadn't poked any holes in it for air and I wondered why we didn't think that was important.

"What's the Good Place like," I asked, slowly bringing the cap down over the mouth of the bottle.

"That's a stupid question," said the angel. "Don't you think so?"

Kavin returned smelling of lemonlime, wiping his hands on his jeans.

"Well?" he said.

"The angel is an asshole," I said.

We both looked at it, looking at us. One of its wings had come off and was slowly sliding down the side of the bottle, sending up a flurry of flakes with every slip.

We agreed to keep it because it might look interesting on the fridge, next to the stabilizer. If it didn't, we could always throw it away.

movie people

The credits slide over them and disappear above their heads. Then Hero shakes out his hair and smiles. Elderly Woman blesses him gently while she sinks her fingers into Heroine's arm and leaves them there. Comedian arrives in an auto and drives Hero and Heroine to their new home. They smile into the breeze like they are destined for a future that involves travelling abroad and speaking English in a casual manner. When they get home, they gaze at the pista green walls, red furniture and posters of shiny Chinese babies. After singing a song about Hero's milk-like heart and Heroine's white face, they fall asleep on a bed that smells like burning plastic. In the middle of the night, Heroine wakes up, smudges her kungkumam, places some jasmine petals on Hero's face and goes back to sleep.

•

Hero wears shirts that match his pants and belts that match his shoes. He drives a pale blue scooter to Office while Heroine stays home to make sambar and chicken. One day Hero announces he is going to America by singing a song about travelling and carrying Heroine around in his eyes, brain, heart and lungs. He leaves the next day and spends the following two weeks with Comedian in a broken shed behind the house. When he comes back, Heroine shows him a seven-year-old boy and a six-year-old girl and says they are his children.

•

The son is violent and moody but everyone loves him because he is a boy. The daughter causes everyone grief because she is a girl who refuses to menstruate early. The children become teenagers in three days. Hero and Heroine hide from them in the puja room and pray to Gods that are unrecognizable but comforting. The daughter disappears and they heave a sigh of relief. The son kidnaps a college girl and locks her in his room. He slaps her repeatedly but she doesn't fall in love with him. When she finally dies of starvation, the son agrees to come out and let Heroine feed him plates of chicken drenched in sambar. He shoves fistfuls of greasy bones into his mouth while Hero and Heroine sing about victorious men with teak-tree bodies and infant hearts.

·

Elderly Woman dies. Hero and Heroine can't remember who she is but go to her house for the funeral so Hero can cry handsomely over her body. The male mourners watch him and feel so sexually aroused that they cry with him. Hero looks at Elderly Woman's possessions and cries handsomely over a desk, which he claims was his grandfather's. While the male mourners fight over who gets to help Hero carry the desk outside, Heroine pulls out the gnarled fingers buried in her forearm. When no one is looking, she stuffs them into Elderly Woman's mouth. When they get home, they place motivational sayings on the alleged grandfather's desk and marvel at what an inspiring man he was.

·

Hero and Heroine's dashing young son turns into a temperamental, gassy middle-aged man overnight. They spend their days replying to spam mails from porn sites, asking if any of the girls would be interested in an alliance with a fair, handsome groom having god-fearing clean and decent habits. One day, while trying to kidnap college girls, they accidentally kidnap Comedian who is now an old man in tight jeans, sunglasses and a shiny black wig. He tells them that their daughter is working as an architect and living with her partner named Elavarasi, but Hero and Heroine insist that they don't know who he is talking about. Comedian says he is late for the last shot of another movie but promises to come back for chicken and sambar. He takes the son along because he says there is some attraction in the boy's personality and walking manner. They all wave to each other, their arms heavy with happiness and hope. Twenty minutes later, Comedian locks the son in the broken shed behind the house and leaves. Hero and Heroine drink hot bottles of sambar and sing an upbeat song about baby boys that are like suns and hearts that turn into kites.

the statue game

Anjali always pointed to her teeth when she tried to sell her appendix. "Canadian teeth," she would say, giving them a tap. "Romba strong. If the teeth are this good then imagine what my appendix must be like."

Unfortunately, nobody wanted to buy her appendix and she couldn't understand this because people in India were buying and selling body parts all the time.

"I don't think there's a market for appendixes," I said. "Try selling your kidneys. Or your liver."

"Why should I? Appendix is just as good as kidneys," she said. "I think I'm being blacklisted because I'm Canadian. If I didn't have this accent I would have sold my appendix a long time ago."

"It's not your accent, it's because you're kind of pink and muscly," I said. "Most Indian women aren't pink and muscly. It makes people suspicious."

I wanted Anjali to go home. I couldn't think of a better place for a Canadian than Canada, but she was very comfortable here. She stayed in a small room down the road from my grandmother's house and spent her time sending postcards to the folks back home. She wrote about how this was a real-deal Indian town that didn't have many cows but there were lots of black pigs and goats that never stopped farting. Water only came out of the taps twice a day and you couldn't drink it because it was filled with malevolent strains of cholera, malaria and small pox. She wrote about how she saw dead rats in the daytime, how people peed at the side of the road, how the electricity came and went as it pleased. Once a month her sister wired her fifty dollars, but Anjali wanted to expand her horizons and you couldn't do that on fifty dollars. This is why she wanted to sell her appendix. One afternoon she came to my grandmother's house and started tugging at the front door.

"What do you want?" I said from the window. I didn't want to let her in because it would take a very long time to put her outside again.

"My sister's coming," she said. "Is the door locked? Why's the door locked?"

"Will she take you back to Canada?"

"I think she's just wants to make sure I'm alright and everything. You know."

"Where are you going to keep her?"

"I was thinking since you've got extra rooms here—"

"No."

"Okay. Well I guess she could stay with me then. I could rent an air conditioner or something. Are you going to open the door?"

"How long is she staying?"

"I don't know. Hey, maybe you could meet her."

"Maybe she'll take you back to Canada," I said.

•

My grandmother died in her sleep in a white Ambassador car, somewhere between Tirunelveli and Nagercoil. When we finished burning her, I was asked to go to her house and settle the "little things", though I wasn't very clear about what these "little things" were. Her house was sparse and mysterious, littered with chairs and straw mats. There was also a broken gramophone player, a cupboard of old silk saris, cooking pots, and a crumbly statue of Krishna that was the size of a small child. He was chipped all over, as if he had been pecked at by millions of tiny birds. Both his hands were missing and there was a large hole where his right knee should have been. His flute had been reduced to a rusted mess of wire that stuck to his cracked lips.

"Give it to me," said Anjali.

"Why?"

"Because I'm totally into Krishna. And it would look really cool in my room."

"Five thousand rupees."

"I'll give you a hundred. Once I sell my appendix."

A builder wasp darted in and out of the hole in Krishna's knee. I wondered what had happened to his hands. It looked like they had been broken off.

"So can I have it?" asked Anjali.

"You can have him for five thousand rupees."

•

The shopkeeper across the street was the custodian of my grandmother's house and the official keeper of the house key. As far as I could tell, he didn't like me for three reasons:

1. I didn't know how to add up my change.
2. I still got "left" and "right" mixed up.
3. I only knew how to count to ten in Tamil.

"I have a question," I said to him one morning. "What can I do with an old statue?"

"Throw it out," said the shopkeeper.

"Isn't it wrong to throw out statues of God?"

"Shouldn't you have mentioned that? How am I to know it's a statue of God?"

"It's a statue of God."

"You need to put it in a river."

"Will you put it in a river for me?"

"No."

"My grandmother would have wanted you to."

"Why are you lying like this?"

"I'm not lying."

"Yes you are."

I went home and sat on the back porch with the statue on my lap. It was the weariest statue of Krishna I had ever seen. The tiny gouges in his eyes made him look vampiric and blind at the same time. His smile seemed to be waiting for the right time to fall off and join the broken hands, wherever they were.

"You remind me of that guy," I said, peering inside the hole in his knee. "The one who couldn't die and they turned him into a grasshopper. Which I never really understood. Why would you turn something into a grasshopper?"

•

I spent my days walking around the house, looking for the little things, carrying the statue on my hip like a broken child. I found wooden boxes shoved under the beds, all of them locked. I wondered what was inside them but was too lazy to try and open them.

"I don't think there are any little things in there," I said. "People don't lock up little things."

I noticed that some rooms had windows that opened into other parts of the house. They were fitted with green and orange glass and the window panes had been painted white then green then brown. I imagined the disappointment of a house guest opening one of these windows, hoping to see the sun or the sky. Instead they would have seen another room, possibly with an old person breathing noisily in a corner. I put Krishna's head next to a window pane.

"There's something very dirty and suspicious about inside windows," I whispered. "Don't you think?"

His head began to rhythmically knock against the pane. It looked like he was trying to split his head open.

"I have a cousin who used to do that all the time when he was small," I said. "I think he still does."

•

It soon became clear that Anjali's sister was not coming on a social visit. She was coming either to take Anjali home or to cut her off because whatever well of affection had spurred her to send fifty dollars a month had completely dried up.

"If I could just sell my appendix I wouldn't give a fuck if she came or not," said Anjali. "She's such an asshole. She's the biggest fucking asshole you ever saw."

I ran my finger along the chips in Krishna's face and hair. Some seemed to have flaked off but there were a number of tiny pits dotting his face like angry, black freckles.

"It's like he was attacked by a bunch of tiny spoons," I said, tapping the gouges in his cheek.

"Let me hold it," said Anjali.

"No."

"For Christ's sake, my sister is going to come here and ruin my fucking life and no one will buy my appendix and I just want to hold the fucking thing, let me hold it."

She held the statue on her lap, then on her hip. She traced his eyebrows and the garland that was melded onto his chest.

"Give it to me," she said. "I mean you don't want it, I'll take it, what's your problem?"

"I have to put it in a river or something. It's very complicated."

"What's so complicated?"

"It's an Indian thing. You wouldn't get it."

"Well fuck that, you think I can't just take it?"

"You know what you should do? Buy yourself a nice Krishna statue. With hands and kneecaps and stuff."

"I think I should just take this one."

"I think you should get your own statue. And then you should go back to Canada."

•

I didn't see Anjali the next day. I asked the shopkeeper if he had seen her and he said he had better things to do than keep track of all the people who came and went in the local vicinity.

"I didn't mean it like that," I said. "I don't think anyone keeps track of things like that. Except maybe the police."

"Was there anything else you wanted?" asked the shopkeeper.

"Do you want to know what else I found in the house?"

"I'm very busy."

"There are all these windows that open into other rooms. I can't understand why anyone would do that. Unless they wanted to spy on each other in a very obvious way."

"If there's nothing else you wanted," he said, pulling out an account ledger. I went home and sat by the window, watching Anjali's house. Then I decided to hide the statue in the old car shed.

"They should ban foreigners from coming here, India makes them crazy," I said, placing him behind the shed door. "They get sunburned and sick and they just go crazy."

I looked up and saw the bats hanging like tiny folded umbrellas from the rafters. I had seen them here before, when I was seven. A boy had rattled a huge bamboo shaft against the rafters, making the bats swish back and forth in the dusty sunlight. I had remained near the doorway, ready to run if they decided to charge us. And here I was, grown up and brave enough to walk in all the way.

"You know, I'm just going to keep you in the house," I said, picking up the statue by the head. I spent the rest of the day sitting at the window. People walked past carrying wire baskets, looking at their watches, talking about how many things had disappointed them recently.

"Why do they do it?" I said. "When they can have barbecues and boyfriends and jobs, why do they come here and make themselves miserable? Although I have heard India is very big with junkies and pedophiles. And spiritualists."

The statue stared blankly out the window, his cold, moulded head leaning against my cheek. He did not seem apprehensive of any of these things, not even of Anjali and the prospect of her pink, muscly arms whisking him away. He wasn't even looking at her house.

•

Anjali reappeared the next evening, reeking of artificial cherries, her eyes angry and slightly unfocused.

"You smell like candy," I said.

"Benadryl. Z-Coff. Somethingsomething," she said. She sat cross-legged on the floor and leaned against the wall. I sat across from her on a plastic chair, holding the statue on my lap.

"I'm going home," she said.

"Good."

"My sister's coming. And we're putting everything in the car. And then we're going home. Do you know what I'll do when I get home?"

"Eat bagels for breakfast. Take your dog to the vet," I said.

"No."

"You'll watch hockey games in bars and drink beer."

"That's so fucking stupid. Is that what you think we do all day?"

"Yes."

"That's so fucking stupid," she said, shaking her head. She stood up, steadying herself against the wall. Then she walked over and placed a finger on the side of Krishna's head.

"What a scummy statue," she said, gently rocking it back and forth.

"Chippy. Not scummy," I said.

"It's fucking scummy. Believe me."

"Well why do you want it if it's so fucking scummy?"

She shrugged and pushed at his head like she was pressing a button. The statue swayed, then slid down and hit the floor with a dull, weary crack. We looked at the pile of broken arms, legs and face.

"Sorry," said Anjali. "I didn't mean to."

She began sweeping up the stray pieces with her foot, pushing a piece of his shoulder with her toe.

"No big deal," she said. "I can buy myself a new one."

•

Anjali left with Krishna's rusted flute sticking out of her back pocket. I collected the remaining pieces, put them in a pista-green plastic bag and walked around the house with the bag hooked over my shoulder. I prodded the locked boxes with my foot and tried to open some of the inside windows, but they were nailed shut. All the nails had been hammered in sloppily and their rusted heads were curled against the window panes like they were sleeping.

"You know what this means, right?" I said. "Someone took a stand against the inside windows. Someone said enough is enough."

I could feel the pieces rolling and shifting against my back. There had been a length of rusted wire in there somewhere and I wondered if it would scratch me and give me tetanus.

The next morning I locked the house and went to the shop across the street.

"Here," I said, sliding the house key across to the shopkeeper.

"You're leaving?" he said. "You've settled everything?"

"Yes," I lied, placing the plastic bag on the counter. "This is the statue I was telling you about," I said.

"I don't want it."

"I'm not giving it to you."

"You can't keep it here."

"I'm not going to. I just want you to know that crazy foreigner girl broke it yesterday. She came in my house and just broke it with her finger. For no reason."

"And what do you want me to do about that?"

"Well I'm just warning you. She might come into your store and break everything. She might just come in and start knocking things down with her finger and then what will you do? Because that's what she did to me," I said.

Half an hour later I was on a bus, sitting beside a woman who repeatedly asked me what time it was, even though I repeatedly told her I had no watch.

"Don't you have a cell phone?" she asked.

"No."

"Why not? My daughter has a cell phone." When her stop came, she brushed past me, leaving behind a heavy space filled with the scent of dead jasmines and vethalai. I placed the bag on the seat where she had been sitting, even though I knew it must be hot and damp and disgusting. Two people came and asked me to move the bag so they could sit down. I said I couldn't and they moved away, muttering bad things about me and my upbringing.

When I was in the auto on the way home, I realized I had left the bag on the bus. For some reason I looked behind me as if I expected to find it there.

"Forgot something?" said the auto driver.

"My bag."

"Your purse? Was there money in it? Cell phone?"

"I don't have a cell phone," I said.

I knew someone would find the bag and open it, possibly with two fingers while they crinkled their nose. Then they would see the clay pieces and say *chee, mannu* and be relieved and disappointed. Or they would see the broken arms and face and say *ada?* Later, when they got to wherever they were going, they would remember this and tell whoever was next to them, *ada, you know what happened on the bus? You know what I found?* They would start a rumor that anti-Hindu factions were leaving broken statues of gods on state buses.

But before all that happened, they would toss the bag out the window, with enough push so that it fell at the side of the road. They would look back to make sure it was really out there and hadn't redoubled inside through the back window or stuck somewhere between their fingers and the atmosphere.

And then they would see it, receding in the dust like it had been there all along with the malnourished water buffalos and clumps of hair.

But she walks away, like the women in commercials
who have just shampooed their hair or bought life insurance
and aren't afraid of dandruff, death or anything.

we will all get better
and then we will get worse

The miracle started as a faint smell that kept shifting into something new and mysterious each day. We made a game of it. We would sniff the air in swirls like we were connoisseurs and say *someone is torching tires in abandoned rice fields. Someone is melting small, pink plastic bags in a cauldron for country liquor purposes.* Two days later we discovered what it was: a rat, bloated and gently bubbling behind a broken suitcase. It had died in its own vomit and as James noticed later, it had left a tiny blood trail through our living room.

"I knew it was a rat," he said as I ran to the bathroom to throw up. "I mean I had a feeling. I had a feeling we had rats."

I wrapped a towel around my nose and went to see what James would do. The rat made him feel empowered and he always did interesting things when he felt empowered. He was waiting for me with a bottle of Vicks.

"Put this on your nose," he said.

"Why?"

"The smell won't be so bad."

"Where'd you learn that?"

"It's what they do here."

James whistled to himself as he draped a rag over the rat and wrapped another around his hands.

"You just saw that on TV or something, didn't you. The Vicks thing."

"I read it in a book," he said as he picked up the rat and went outside. James always seemed jarringly out of place in the bright sun. He crouched down, pretending that the soil was used to him. The rat was soon hidden under a moist scar in the ground, cloth and all.

"You know what this is?" he said. "It's a miracle."

"That's not a miracle," I said.

"Sure it is. We found the rat all by ourselves. We didn't have to call anybody. Nobody charged us 300 bucks to get rid of it."

"Nobody charges 300 rupees to get rid of rats."

"I'm just saying. I mean we did this ourselves. If it happens again, we can handle it ourselves. We'll be okay."

"I'm going to lie down," I said, turning to go inside.

"You did great," James called after me. "We both did great."

•

We started talking about miracles regularly after that because I felt James didn't really understand what a miracle was. If I was in a generous mood, I would explain that life was a miracle. Sugar was a miracle. But usually I wasn't in a generous mood and I would poke him in the chest and say,

Water is a miracle, James.

It's a miracle to have clean, clear water to drink when you're thirsty.

It's a miracle to be able to open your water pot or refrigerator if you have one (which is another miracle altogether) and find water there that you can drink.

And if you don't have drinking water, it's a miracle to have four squares of peanut candy.

It's a miracle that four squares of peanut candy is all you need to make hard water go down like real water.

That is a fucking miracle, James.

The more I thought about it, the more miracles I felt compelled to explain to him. It was a miracle I hadn't contracted a fungal infection from my anaemia. It was a miracle we could still afford to buy coffee.

"I think we're a miracle," he said.

"Babies, James," I said, poking him in the neck. "Babies are miracles."

"Imagine if we had babies."

"We'd eat them."

"No we wouldn't. I wouldn't."

"We'd sell them to Americans. I heard they pay a lot for pretty Indian babies."

"You think our babies would be pretty?"

I sighed and shook my head.

"No. They would probably be ugly. On purpose."

•

The next day, James suggested we take an evening walk. He always walked with his shoulders squared, his chest slightly puffed out so that he looked like a duck waddling with a great sense of purpose along the gravel stretch of road. I would tug at his arm, trying to collapse him a bit but he would just wink and sing *Nenja thooki naddra naddra* over and over. He always took me by the hand and forced me to walk beside him, which never worked because I always lagged a bit behind.

"I have a blister on the back of my leg," said James, yanking me forward.

"And?"

"It'll go away."

We walked until we reached the broken bridge that arched over a dark, scummy pond. The surface was covered with a thin, grey web of mosquitoes.

"It's a miracle we haven't died from malaria and dengue fever," I said.

"It's a miracle that I used to be a miracle," said James. "When I was small, I mean. My grandmother prayed especially for me."

"Prayer baby."

"Why are you saying that like it's a bad thing?"

"You're not a miracle now."

"You know what happens when you talk bitter? Your upper lip disappears. Completely."

I leaned over and gazed at the dark water. James began rubbing the back of his leg against a broken chunk of the bridge.

"What are you doing?" I said.

"It's that blister, it itches."

"That's disgusting."

James shrugged and kept grating his leg against the crumbling concrete.

•

The next morning, the first thing I saw was James sitting cross-legged on the bed. He thrust his fist into my face, his fingers opening slowly like a flower. Lying in his palm was something that looked like the skeleton of a tiny hand.

"Is that part of the rat? Did you dig it up?" I said.

"No," he said, shaking his head slowly. "Is that what it looks like?"

"I don't know—did you find it in the kitchen or something?"

"It was in that blister."

I noticed that his palm and fingers were lightly streaked with dried blood.

"That's gross, James," I said.

"You think so? I think it's kind of neat. Have you ever had anything come out of a blister before?" He was looking at his palm, the tip of his tongue poking out between his teeth. "I bet you haven't," he said quietly.

"So?"

"That's probably why you don't get why it's neat."

His finger seemed awkwardly large, splotched with red and brown. The tiny skeleton looked like it was about to shatter.

"It's probably calcium deposits. Or phosphorous. The body pushes stuff out like that all the time," I said.

"I don't think it's phosphorous."

"It's detritus. It's like sweat."

"Detritus," said James, rolling the word around in his mouth. I could almost hear it crash against the back of his teeth.

•

The plan had been that James would go into town and do a "big shopping" because there was hardly anything to eat in the house. But now he had pulled a chair next to the window and was examining his arms and legs for more blisters. As the morning progressed he began finding them on his arms, chest and legs. He would say *Ha!* each time he found one, followed by a series of muffled *ha-ha-ha*s as he examined the blister closely. He scratched at all of them—if he didn't say anything that meant the blister was empty. If he said *motherFUCKER* that meant something had been in the blister. If he said *Otha Mayire* that meant he had to tweeze whatever it was out but it had come out eventually and he was the winner. I stayed in the other room, finishing the last of the biscuits and jam. I searched the cupboards, trying to find something else to eat but there was nothing but a bottle of mouldy peanuts.

"When are you going?" I called out to him.

"Come here, come here," he called back. "Come see."

I went to the doorway and leaned against it, refusing to go inside the room. James seemed to be glowing with sticky streaks and raw, pink smudges. On the floor, arranged in neat rows on a piece of paper, was a collection of tiny bones. I could see a small foot and something that looked like a spinal column.

"Look at that," he said grinning. "I bet this never happened to you. I bet you've never even had blisters, have you?"

"Maybe you're sick or something. Maybe you've got an infection."

"Imagine if this happened to you. You'd—I can't even imagine what you'd do."

"So you're not going then?"

"Where?"

"There's nothing to eat."

"You want me to go shopping? Like this?"

He held out his arms, stretching them slowly, in case I couldn't understand what he was trying to say.

•

I spent the afternoon in the front room, looking at the road, clutching the big-shopping money in my hand. James always did the big shopping because he was less likely to get cheated than I was. I would pay whatever the vendors asked because I didn't want them to hate me. James explained that it didn't work that way. If you didn't fight over the price they would think you were stupid.

"What would you do if I wasn't here?" he asked me once.

"What do you mean?"

"How would you buy stuff? How would you survive?"

"I'd sell my ovaries for rice. Home delivery."

"I don't think anyone would want your ovaries."

"Not even you?"

"Not even me."

I took a deep breath and separated the big-shopping money, notes in the left hand, coins in the right.

You can do this, I said to myself. *You know why? Because everyone can do this. And everyone includes you. So. Just*

open the front gate,
close it,
open the black umbrella,
walk up to the main road,
stop a rickshaw,
argue with the driver about the price,
watch him shake his head and drive away,

I couldn't get past this part. *You keep walking,* I told myself. *You'll find another rickshaw,* but I just saw myself standing there at the side of the road, sweating under my black umbrella. *Or take the fucking bus. Take the bus and die of panic. Scar yourself for the next few months.*

In the other room, James had spent a productive afternoon taking a long bath and dousing himself in prickly heat powder. He was sitting with a towel wrapped around his waist, humming to himself.

"What have you been doing?" he asked.

"Nothing."

"You're always doing nothing."

"Found any more?"

"Nope. I think they're gone now. Whatever they were."

"I'm pretty sure they were just some kind of heat boils or something."

I realized that I was still clutching the big-shopping money in my hand. The notes had become damp and grimy.

"I thought I would go shopping," I said.

"I'll go tomorrow. I'll be alright tomorrow."

"There's nothing to eat."

"I'm not hungry."

"I am."

In order to make up for my hunger, James decided to sleep on the floor that night. He spread out a straw mat at the foot of the bed and a thin white cloth over it. Tiny clouds of powder fell like snow whenever he moved. I noticed that the blood-stained paper was still on the floor, scattered and speckled with the small yellow bones.

"It's like your body was spitting out some tiny animal in bits and pieces." I said. "Or a baby. A really small baby."

James suddenly started to chuckle.

"What?" I said.

"I was thinking about what you said. About babies."

"What did I say?"

"That we'd eat them if we had them."

"I was right," I said. "You ate them and now you're spitting them out."

•

It was still dark when I woke up. The electricity had gone and I was drenched in sweat, the hum of mosquitoes covering my head like a thick blanket. James was holding a candle, looking down at his hand.

"What are you doing?" I said.

The back of his hands were rippled with blisters. Some of them seemed to be fused together while others were piling and growing on top of each other.

"Take me to the doctor," he whispered.

"They're just heat boils Jamesy."

"I don't think these are heat boils."

His eyes were shimmering and looked like they were about to run down his face.

"I'd just feel much better if I saw a doctor," he said.

I sighed and began running my fingers through his hair.

"You know it'll cost about 200 rupees though, right?" I said as the sweaty clumps of his hair slipped through my fingers. "And 75 for an auto. And meds will be a couple hundred, even if we cut out painkillers and vitamins. So I'm thinking around 500 bucks we'll need. You have 500 bucks?"

James didn't say anything. He was looking at his arms, turning them slowly in the candle light.

"It's heat boils Jamesy. Just leave them alone and you'll be fine. Okay?"

In the morning, James would not get up. The blisters had spread along the inside of his arm like shiny, silent hills. He lay on his back, looking up at the ceiling, his lips drying and discolouring in the heavy heat. I sat beside him, tracing a design in the straw mats.

"Would you feel better if you popped one? I don't think anything would happen if you popped just one. Maybe it will cheer you up."

He shook his head. The blood-stained paper was still lying patiently at the side of the room. The bones seemed to have shifted a little, like someone had examined them when we were sleeping.

"Do you have any?" he asked.

"No."

"Did you check your back?"

"I don't have any."

"Let me check your back," he said, getting up. I pulled off my top and turned around. I could feel his fingers passing lightly over my skin, tracing and touching invisible, incomplete shapes. It reminded me of a game couples were supposed to play—*What am I writing? No, just guess. Come on.* I felt a sharp, sloppy stab as his nails bit into the middle of my back, slowly, in three hard lines that kept sliding to the left, then right. I turned around and looked at James.

"There was one," he said.

"No there wasn't," I said, pulling my top back on.

I spent the morning double-checking all the cupboards and drawers, looking for abandoned pieces of candy. I found some old coconut oil in a bottle I thought was empty. *Coconut oil is fat and protein and natural vegetable oils,* I thought. *Nut oils. Not vegetable. It's all natural goodness, right from the bottle. Go on, have a drinkie-winkie.*

"Where's my shirt?" James was standing in the doorway. He had his mouth open, which made him look like he was drunk. His eyes looked larger and darker than usual.

"Why?" I asked.

"I'm going to the doctor. If you won't take me I'll go myself."

"I'll take you in the evening Jamesy. Promise," I said.

"No you won't."

"I will. I can."

He looked at the floor and frowned.

"No you won't," he said and slipped out of the doorway. I heard him enter the bedroom, then the creak of the bed as he sat down on it. Or maybe he lay down. I hid the coconut oil behind a plate so he wouldn't find it.

•

I sat in the front room, in the big chair that James usually sat in.

Now, I said to myself. *Let's try this again.*

Open the front gate,

close it,

open the black umbrella,

walk up to the main road,

stop a rickshaw.

What if there are no rickshaws on the main road?

Well let's think hypodermically.

Hypothetically.

Let's say, by some miracle, that there is a line of rickshaws just waiting for you at the road. And guess who's in the first one?

Hypothetically,

miraculously,

it is Rajinikanth.

And you are so happy you start crying because Rajinikanth is a miracle. And he flips his cigarette and tells you to get in—no charge of course. And you head home, with all the other autos following in a line. And they are all singing songs of patriotism and strength that make you feel happy and filled with possibilities. They all carry James out and he looks pale and broken like a raped woman from the movies and you look up at Rajinikanth and say I didn't think anyone would come.

And he says,

Aabathil vidamaaten

Veyilo puyal mazhaiyo

Maatennu sollamaaten

And everyone will take James to the doctor and he'll say James was just being an ass, picking at his heat boils and there is nothing wrong with him. So there will be no charge and in the meantime all the other rickshaw drivers will do the big shopping and buy everything we need for nothing because rickshaw drivers are miracles.

I opened my hand, to make sure the big-shopping money was still there. The notes seemed to be getting dirtier while the coins seemed shinier, flashing brilliantly in the sun like buttons of light.

In conclusion, in all hypodermic hypotheticalness, it is only logical to assume that you can in fact really do this, I said to myself. *And I know you can do it. It will be like sugar and babies. It will be like drinking water.*

Open the front gate,
close it,
open the black umbrella,
walk up to the main road,
hail a rickshaw.

Do the big shopping with your elbows out, nenja thooki naddra naddra, *but not so much because you are a woman and shouldn't make others aware of your chest.*

Find fifteen doctors filled with explanations for tiny bones who will come home and cure James of his miracles.

You are going to do it all.
You can do it.

I sank deeper into the chair, feeling the plastic armrests rise up beside me like friends filled with confidence, like bodyguards.

You can do it.

shapeshifters

The shapeshifter and I play carrom in the afternoon. I eat toast with pepper while the shapeshifter sinks coins like it's no big deal and gives me tips on how to be a better me.

"You have to stop being depressed first," says the shapeshifter.

"I'm not depressed," I say, frowning at the board.

"You are," says the shapeshifter. "That's why you're like this."

"Like what?"

"No job. Unmarried. Fat also."

I call the shapeshifter an asshole and the shapeshifter turns into Ms. Bradley, my music teacher from grade six. She smiles fiercely under a crown of bright blonde hair, her high heels stabbing into the meek floor. She accuses me of being an ugly brown girl who turned all the white students into racists. She also accuses me of tracking up the carpet with my muddy shoes, impregnating her husband, and stealing all her HB pencils.

"Someone once told me that ugly brown girls turn into unicorns," I say. "Isn't that so stupid? Ugly brown girls don't turn into anything."

"Sure they do," says the shapeshifter. "They can turn into great conversationalists if trained properly."

"But not unicorns, right?"

"No," says the shapeshifter as Ms. Bradley's blonde hair begins to crystallize around her face. "Ugly brown girls can't turn into unicorns."

•

When we get bored with carrom, the shapeshifter turns into seven purple chicks. I feed them stale bread crumbs and explain how coloured chicks are usually very sick but you only learn about this later, when you've already paid for them and brought them home.

"Ugly brown girls turn into coloured chicks," says the shapeshifter.

"That's so stupid," I say. "That's even stupider than the unicorn thing."

The shapeshifter says that a vegan diet and raising plants could definitely help in combatting my depression. It also suggests that I avoid wearing light colours and make more of an effort to meet new people.

"If I was a shapeshifter," I say, "I would probably turn into something exotic. Like a hobbit. Or a white guy."

"You probably wouldn't turn into anything."

"You don't know that," I say. "I might turn into a unicorn. I might turn into a white guy and a unicorn at the same time. And a hobbit. I might turn into a whiteguyhobbitcorn."

The shapeshifter says that now I'm just being disrespectful, so I apologize. I ask the shapeshifter to turn into a white guy but it says it can't if it's upset or if someone is watching. It promises to turn into a hobbit for me another time, when it isn't feeling so tired.

•

We play Scrabble for a while but stop when the shapeshifter starts to lose. We think about playing carrom again but the expanse of the board and the drifts of white powder make us feel tired and lonely. The shapeshifter says that it sometimes feels homesick, but won't say where home is. It halfheartedly turns into an old shoe, a small dog, a clutch of dying moths. It asks if I'm getting bored and I say yeah, a little.

"Boredom is a sure sign of depression," says the shapeshifter. "You should read more. And drink lots of water. You should do abdominal exercises."

"You know what I used to think? When I was little?" I say. "I used to think that if I gave myself enough surface burns, the scars would make me turn white."

"And?"

"And then Ms. Bradley would like me."

"Wow."

"Yeah. I also used to think that poo came out of your butt cheeks."

I start feeling hungry and say that I should probably be going soon. The shapeshifter does not ask me to stay and I wonder what it plans to do after I'm gone. At the door, it shifts into a bouquet of purple flowers which I can look at for a while but can't take home.

"Try the vegan diet and tell me how it goes," says the shapeshifter. "And remember to think positive. Think positive and drink lots of water."

As I walk home, I decide that if I really tried, I could probably turn into a unicorn. The only reason I haven't yet is because I don't want to.

the party house

The house is ugly. The street dogs scattered in front of it are handsome and the road leading up to the house sparkles under the sodium lights. But the house itself is ugly and Shalini and Tina and I feel glad that we don't know who lives here. We pass the handsome dogs and enter the ugly house because the Telugu guy needs to meet someone for five minutes and then we are leaving.

"Five minutes," says the Telugu guy and we say okay, no problem, sure. We wait for him in the kitchen where a cockroach is running round the rim of a bowl of vegetable soup. Youngsters with accents and faces like heavy cream stumble in and ask where the party is.

"This is the party, son," says Shalini, like she is from Kansas or something, like she has always called people "son". The youngsters walk through to the living room and do not come out again. This makes Shalini believe we are in one of those whorehouses that have chunkywhite English-speaking girls from Mumbai who fuck you for very less money.

"How much very less money?" I ask.

"Like very much less," says Shalini. "Like, eight hundred rupees or something."

We momentarily feel bad for these chunkywhite English-speaking girls from Mumbai and hope they will go for computer classes and get better jobs in the future. We try to set fire to the cockroach with Tina's pink lighter. Then we send her to look for the Telugu guy. She comes back and says everyone wants us to come into the living room because they don't want us sitting in the kitchen anymore.

•

The living room is filled with youngsters. There are also some masala peanuts, old New Year's cards and a rexine sofa but mostly there are youngsters. We decide they all look the same and talk funny. Shalini says we are racist against youngsters and Tina says hey ChiranjeeviNagarjuna ayipointha, can we go now and the Telugu guy says five minutes ma. We sit beside a homeless guy called Vinay who keeps telling us how homeless he is. He tells us that he sleeps on the pavement and is friends with drug dealers and auto drivers because they are people too, even though they are drug dealers and auto drivers. He tells us he has malaria and it's pretty sweet. Malaria is a sweet disease, he says. He is also writing a novel, which an agent in America has already shown interest in.

"You're very clean for a homeless person," says Shalini. "And you speak English well. I usually can't understand what homeless people say. Because they're always like 'ammaamma', you know? Ammaammaamma."

"Those are beggars," says Vinay. "Beggars are different."

"Amma," says Tina. "Amma, amma. Amma."

It rains. It stops raining. The Telugu guy tells someone to forward him their pertinants. A girl shows Shalini her tattoo and Shalini says it looks like a sea of green vomit. Homeless Vinay goes home, which he apparently does three times a week to shower and check email. It looks like there are fewer youngsters than there were before. Shalini says they must be in the rooms, fucking the chunkywhite English-speaking girls from Mumbai, making sounds like dying animals because youngsters make a lot of noise when they fuck.

"Because it's still exciting for them you know?" says Shalini. "It's still exciting for them to see boobies or a peepee."

The ugly house sits and stares at us, waiting for us to go home. The remaining youngsters drape themselves over the rexine sofa, kiss each other like they are sharing secrets, ask us what time it is. Tina says there are people here who were born in 1990.

"What does that even mean?" she says. "How can people be born in 1990?"

Then she says she wants to fuck a chunkywhite English-speaking girl from Mumbai too.

"Or I want to watch," she says, standing up. "I want to hear what it sounds like."

Shalini and I wait for her to sit down again. But she walks away, like the women in commercials who have just shampooed their hair or bought life insurance and aren't afraid of dandruff, death or anything.

when the other girls come

The wall beside the bed is plastered with tiny stickers of Muruga. Whoever was here before me lined them up very neatly, and wrote "Om Muruga Thunai" underneath them, once in Tamil and once in English. I imagine a girl with flaky skin and ovarian cysts, her fingers lightly touching the stickers as she thinks of how lucky she is to have found this pg accommodation at just threefive a month, breakfast and dinner with teacoffee, lunch provided on Sundays. I trace the edges of the stickers and decide to pick them off tomorrow morning. When the other girls come, I will say "Hi excuse me. You know who stayed in this bed prior? See, they have put all these stickers like this. I find such behavior really so annoying, don't you agree?"

I sit cross-legged on my bed and wait for them. Then I walk quickly around the room to get my exercise. It is important for single women who are staying independently to get plenty of exercise. They should also eat fresh fruits and vegetables whenever possible, and sit beside a window at least once a day. The window in this room is a tiny square of weak, milky light, but it will be nice to sit here with the other girls when they come. I look over the room with the confidence of a single woman who stays independently. Coils of grey hair stand in quiet pools in the corners. Some strands are piled against the wall like they are sleeping. One of the girls staying here must be a woman. She must be a spinster who combs her hair, knots the fallen strands together and throws it on the floor because she is very bitter about her life and family. I will not talk to her. I will be polite but I will not talk to her.

•

The bathroom floor is dry. When I open the tap, it gives a raspy whistle that makes me feel thirsty. Wisps of grey hair have wrapped themselves around the pipes and there is a cement imprint of a tiny hand right at the top of the bathroom door. I sit on the washing stone and wait for the water to come. I know it will come because this place has 24hourswater. I once stayed in a hostel where the 24hourswater came every other day for an hour in the afternoon. One afternoon, a girl came out of a bathing stall, her bucket brimming with damp twists of washed clothes. Fat lines of rusty blood were inching out of her nose and disappearing between her lips.

"Are you okay?" I asked.

"Hello," she said. I watched her walk down the hall and disappear into the folds and shadows of her room.

The bathroom stall becomes dim as it grows dark outside. I decide that the water will come tomorrow and go back to my room. I decide to ask the girls about the water timings when they come. I sit on my bed and wait for them. Then I fall asleep with my hand against the wall, my fingers lightly touching the Muruga stickers beside my head. I dream of the other girls. They enter the room in single-file, talking about how lucky we all are to have a pg accommodation at just threefive a month, breakfast and dinner with teacoffee, lunch provided on Sundays. They sit cross-legged on my bed and look at me with eyes that are soft coils of grey hair. Stray strands hang from the corners of their mouths, waving forlornly in the stale breeze of the fan.

"We're so lucky to have found this place," I say. "So lucky."

I wait for the dream to end so I can wake up and tell the other girls all about it, when the other girls come.

put your hand
in the hand
of the man
with his hand
in the hand
of the man
with his hand
in the windmills
of your mind

Picture a McIntosh apple pulling away from your seven-year-old mouth. In the background, breakdancers spin their faces on contraband pieces of cardboard. The McIntosh has one of your teeth embedded in its pulp. *I put that there,* you think. *I did that.*

> *Yo man*
> *what do you expect,*
> *the guy's a gigolo, man!*
> *Youknowhaimean?*

Picture you picturing a McIntosh apple stuffed with broken teeth that snake around the cores like spare change. *A rich source of calcium, consonants and quarters but don't eat the skin because it will serrate your stomach lining and you will bleed to death without even knowing it.* You hurl the apple into the air and you wait for it to come down and you don't really care when it doesn't.

Picture a boy who likes the Eurythmics. He talks about a hotel with revolving doors that lead into swirling yellow nitrogen storms. He is unsure of what lies beyond these storms though he thinks there could be mutant panthers or abandoned ice cream trucks. He insists this is not about magic.

I like to.
Listen to.
Beethoven.

Picture a dream where this boy's fingers are secretly locked over your lungs. He sits in class with the stubs of his hands looking like melting apples, the skins falling off in messy, red strands. He asks if anyone has seen his fingers but everyone says no.

Picture a summer with no apples because of pesticides that may cause children to turn into fish when they are thirty-seven years old. The sky is pockmarked with cancer-enriched sunlight. You are not allowed outside, not because of the cancer but because you are brown enough as it is.

Julie Gerond
with the golden blonde hair
rides the polka-dot pony
at the summer-long fair

Picture you picturing Julie Gerond at the summer-long fair. Strangers ask if they can take her picture and she laughs and says *oh my God, are you serious? This is so embarrassing, are you serious? Are you for real? Okay, sure I guess, I mean, are you serious? Oh my God!* Someone gives her a tub of strawberry ice cream which just sits there in the heat of the summer-long fair but doesn't melt.

Picture a mouthbreather who decorates the church parking lot with drawings of nuclear reactor signs that look like windmills. You are sure she has killed someone, possibly with a short knife or a plastic bag. *I'm not smart,* says the mouthbreather. *But I'm super-talented.*

Pie Jesu Domine,
dona eis requiem

She tells you she is allergic to everything, even apples. If she eats an apple, her throat will swell up. You believe that McIntoshes would be exceptionally deadly, causing her eyes to melt into slicks of silver. Tiny blue birds with scissors for beaks would appear on the rims of her eye sockets but you don't tell her any of this.

Picture a McIntosh apple spinning silently in space. This nutritious yet delicious snack takes twenty-three years to smash into your right temple where it imbeds broken teeth into your brain like old, violent friends.

Since I left Plumtree,
down in Tennessee,
it's the first time
I've been warm

Right before the end, you meet someone who looks a lot like Annie Lennox but not really. *And now, for the absolute win,* she says. *What is borborygmi?* It's a kind of hobbit, you say. It is characterized by a disposition to sing the Rolling Stones for no reason. In certain cultures, it is regarded as a demon. Not-Really-Annie-Lennox says no but she says it kindly, like it doesn't really matter and so it doesn't hurt that much.

"I don't know what's wrong," said Kalaiselvi, shaking her head. "Everything is so hard to do."

six things we found during the autopsy

1. PLAYBOY

A Playboy was hidden behind her jaw, rolled and bent like she had stashed it there in a hurry. Black and white alarm clocks were pasted over the women's breasts and the words !wUt aLarming bOobeez! were scrawled across the stomachs. It was hard to tell if she had done this herself or if someone else had done it for her.

We could not find any incisions so we decided she must have rammed the Playboy into her ear and hoped for the best. We thought this made her stoic, medically marvellous and gay. We wondered if she had a secret crush on one of us and while we unanimously agreed that this was possible, we knew in our hearts that it was not.

2. BLACK ANTS

The ants were an ongoing observation, like watching fish. They floated up gently through her skin, broke the surface and lay there like the journey had made them tired and they just needed to lie down for a while. We discovered that there were no ants near her elbows but could not come to a consensus as to how this was significant. We thought we saw something that resembled an abnormally thick spiderweb under her pancreas and decided not to pursue that line of inquiry because it obviously had nothing to do with the ants.

We wondered if she had let the ants in or if they had smashed their way through her, vandalizing her body with starred and spangled railroads, towers and pornography. Now that she was dead, the ants probably had no reason to stay. We thought this was heartbreaking but also the best option for everyone involved.

3. ANGELS

The angels were clustered and nested behind her heart and lungs. They had to be pulled out with tweezers, which was not easy because they kept hanging onto her esophagus with their angry fingers and teeth. They had no nipples, bellybuttons or genitalia, which made them like dolls but we did not feel like combing their hair. Their feet looked like hands and they dug their heels into our faces as a sign of protest. They caterwauled. They sounded like prehistoric birds that were heartbroken because they were going to die in the evening.

We thought she must have been a closeted Catholic. We thought she had probably been more into the angels than she was into Jesus, which is why she had allowed them to stay in such a communally sensitive area. We thought it was racist to assume that only Catholics had an affinity for angels.

4. ST. SEBASTIAN

St. Sebastian was tied to her spinal column, eyes looking heavenward, an arrow running into his chin and out of his forehead. His body was peppered with arrows but it was the one through his forehead that made us untie him. We thought that untying him would make him feel better. We didn't touch the arrow because we thought it would make his head fall off.

We thought the angels and St. Sebastian were probably good friends. We imagined them hanging out in the late afternoon, folding discarded angel wings into boats and sailing them on her bloodstream, hoping they would return filled with things that were sweet and useful.

5. TYPHOID

It was only later, when we were delirious, sour-mouthed and tired, that we realized we all had typhoid. While we waited for it to go away, we cleverly and calculatingly deduced where we got it from. The typhoid was a shiny black slab that was stuck to the back of her liver. It came apart in layers but could not be removed completely.

We thought she was a typhoid carrier. We thought she had probably infected all of us and the typhoid was sticking to our livers too. We decided that we were angry at the world and this was what people with cancer felt like. We thought it must be a neat thing to be a typhoid carrier.

6. PLAYGIRL

The Playgirl was spread across her ribcage like a placemat. Hairless, half-aroused men stared sexingly into our faces and we looked at their half-arousal and sighed. We pasted the heads of Siberian Huskies onto their faces and decided this made them more regal and less attainable. We also decided that if we ever created a pantheon of Gods, there would be a set of twins who would be bare-chested and Siberian Husky-headed.

We knew she was the only one who could have made it with a hairless, half-aroused Playgirl man with a Siberian Husky head. We imagined it happening in a series of well-lit photographs where she and the Playgirl man were naked and open-mouthed but not sweating. We contrasted the open Playgirl with the rolled and bent Playboy and decided that she had been conflicted about her sexuality. We thought we could have been the awesome friends who held her hand while we dragged her out of the closet. We thought we could have convinced her it was okay to like girls even if she didn't like any of us.

we will speak about
brain aneurysms

My uncle will have a brain aneurysm. My uncle who goes to Kenya and Nairobi and has overdosed two dogs with liver medicine will probably not know what a brain aneurysm is, but he will have one anyway. He will have it in front of a handful of bored students, in a college auditorium that smells like kerosene and urine. There is a chance that before my uncle has his aneurysm he will have headaches, nausea or vomiting, which he will diagnose as viral fever. He will take a Crocin, put cotton in his ears, shove enthusiastic portions of Vicks up his nose. There is a chance that he will also take his pancreas revitalizing tonic, because he believes that all his ailments are a result of a faulty pancreas. My uncle has irritable bowels, wheezing, and an angry tangle of love for his wife that sits on top of his stomach and gives him indigestion every night. He believes the pancreas revitalizing tonic is fixing everything, filling him with pancreatic strength and vitality.

My uncle will have his brain aneurysm right in the middle of his lecture. Sometimes I will tell people that he started repeating the word "hentai" while talking about the effects of pesticide use on hybrid strains of rice. Sometimes I will say that he started wandering around the stage, asking if the Chozhan Express was late again. This is because I will not really know what happened. The bored students will probably decide he is drunk, because that is something people often assume about my uncle when he is talking or doing nothing. They will probably remember the whole thing as "the drunk lecture", even after they learn about the brain aneurysm.

My uncle will not be taken to a hospital. Someone, possibly a sweaty final-year student wearing his best shirt tucked into his jeans in honour of the special guest lecture, will put my uncle on a train and send him home. My uncle will sit among moist, tired families and dusty luggage while blood leaks into his brain. Later, I will try and imagine what this feels like. I will decide that it is like the blunt force trauma they show on TV. I will think of white people gasping prettily in pain and decide that I know exactly what a brain aneurysm is.

My uncle will die in a hospital, on the very afternoon that everyone is away doing other things. His wife and daughter will believe he did this on purpose, but won't say anything until a suitable amount of time has passed. His pancreas revitalizing tonic will be dumped in the garden and stain the ground purple. Later, when people ask us about our family, we will speak about brain aneurysms. We will furrow our brows like he never existed and move our mouths like we know what we are talking about.

throwing rocks at dogs

Kalaiselvi saw them when she was walking home. They were hanging around a tamarind tree, their tiny black eyes darting back and forth. It was the same bunch that had tried to open her front gate last week. She had yelled at them, her hands banging ineffectually at the window as they sauntered away laughing. They looked exactly the same. They were wearing the same clothes; the same stains clung to their dirty faces and arms.

As soon as she got home, Kalaiselvi went to the garden and found a stone that fit comfortably inside her fist. Then she crouched by her window and waited. It was the small one that finally entered; the one with sagging blue shorts. The stone whipped silently through the air and caught the small boy in the side of the head. She watched as he crumpled to the ground; then she waited for him to jump to his feet and run. But he didn't.

•

Kalaiselvi locked the gate and dragged the little body inside. She wrapped her hands in plastic bags first because it was a slum boy and she knew that the safest way to touch slum boys was with plastic bags on your hands. She grabbed his bony ankles, pulled him into the front room and locked the door. His shorts clung awkwardly to his hips and a filthy rope of red thread snaked over his bloated stomach. He was bald, with a scar above one eyebrow and tiny cuts around his mouth. Kalaiselvi picked up the phone, dialed and waited with her lips slightly pursed. She heard a click, then a man's voice that sounded like steel wool.

"Adhi?" she said.

"What?" said the man.

"I think you should come here," said Kalaiselvi.

"What for?"

"I've done something."

•

Kalaiselvi used to spend a lot of time thinking of Adhi's voice. She said this was because it did not fit his face or body, which were both rather unremarkable.

"But your voice," she said to him one day, "is like beedi smoke in the morning, right after the rain, when it's still cloudy."

"Is that a good thing?" he said.

"It's the most gorgeous thing in the world," said Kalaiselvi, grinding her knuckles into his forearm. She was always grinding her knuckles into some part of him, saying he was like wet cement on a hot day, like manvaasanai, like a fresh wound in a green coconut. One day when they were travelling by bus it rained, suddenly and fiercely from a sky that was as dark as ink. Just as suddenly, the rain stopped and the sun split the sky with a single yellow beam. Kalaiselvi had leaned forward, breathing in everything with her mouth half open. Adhi felt her knuckles grind into his thigh, like she was carving a hole into his skin, right to the bone.

•

Adhi came seven and a half minutes after Kalaiselvi phoned. She heard him find the key under the rug and open the door. She pictured him staring down at the little boy lying on the floor.

"Who is this," he asked when she entered.

"One of those slum boys. He snuck in and tried to steal something. I hit him in the head with a rock."

He looked at her, his eyebrows gently furrowing and straightening out, as if the realization was only hitting him in ebbs and waves.

"It's like throwing rocks at dogs, Adhi. It's no different," Kalaiselvi said.

"This is not a dog," he said, kneeling down. "This is a boy."

Adhi checked for a pulse and heartbeat. Then he checked if the boy was breathing.

"I think you just knocked him out. You want me to take him to the doctor?"

"No," said Kalaiselvi. "Wait with me until he wakes up."

"Then what?"

"Then you can go."

They sat at opposite corners of the room, alternately looking out the window and at the boy. Adhi said the slum would be after her now. Angry men and women with coarse brown hair and bright red mouths would beat down her door, demanding money because she had stoned one of their boys. They would come after her for the rest of her life. Kalaiselvi began to laugh.

"What can they possibly take?" she said, looking at the room. "They can take my coconut brooms. Both of them. They can take my chappals."

"When he wakes up we can say he fainted or something," said Adhi. "We can give him a glass of milk and send him home. Do you have any milk?"

"They were just standing there, a bunch of them, watching me, waiting to sneak in here and steal something. They think I'm an idiot. They think they can just walk in here and take whatever they want. Why would they do that? I don't have anything to take."

"You don't have to give him any milk," said Adhi. "Not if you don't want to."

•

Kalaiselvi was down to two meals a day. She had four sets of clothes and one pair of chappals that people kept mistaking for bathroom chappals. You've worn your bathroom chappals outside, they would say with a chuckle and she would shake her head solemnly and say no, these are my good chappals. These are all I have. When the vendors cheated her out of a few extra rupees, she made it a point to tell them that she knew what they had done. She would show them the holes in her clothes and say look at this. Just because I can speak English does not mean you can cheat me. At least you should be fair.

"It's hard for me to do ordinary things," she had told Adhi one day. "It took me ten years to get my ration card and they spelt everything wrong—my name, the street name, everything. I have to go all the way to Kattumannarkoil to get it changed. Everyone else on this street got their ration card in six months with no spelling mistakes. And they don't even need their ration cards!"

This affected her greatly, the fact that her neighbours had perfect ration cards that sat quietly in large steel cupboards. None of them bought ration sugar. One lady bought ration rice but used it to feed her dog.

"I don't know what's wrong," said Kalaiselvi, shaking her head. "Everything is so hard to do."

Adhi had gone with her to Kattumannarkoil, waited with her in the decaying government office, listened to her explain to the peon that she had no money for a bribe and watched as the peon gently sneered and told her to come back tomorrow. That's when Adhi had cornered him and whispered "Thevidiya payan, you want something? You want me to give you something?"

A few minutes later, Kalaiselvi was putting her papers inside her yellow cloth bag while Adhi waited for her in the street.

"If you ever come this side again, just see what happens to your ration card," said the peon from the doorway. "Just see what I do to you."

On the bus ride home, Adhi's anger seemed to fall into itself, eating away at his heart and stomach.

"It doesn't matter," said Kalaiselvi. "The rice is always damp and mouldy. And have you seen the sugar? It's yellow. Sometimes it's brown. I don't eat that much sugar anyway. Sugar's bad for you. It gives you diabetes."

Adhi suddenly felt too tired to say anything.

•

The slum boy's hand twitched. His grubby forefinger extended, like he was anxiously pointing at something. Then it curled into itself like a dying worm.

"What do you think his name is?" said Kalaiselvi.

"Ramesh. Satish. John Pandian," said Adhi.

Kalaiselvi looked at him with her head tilted to the side.

"I just realized your name is very slum," she said.

"No it's not."

"Yes it is. It's like a hit man's name. It's like Veera. Or Rockappan."

"It's short for Adhinarayanan."

"Are you serious?"

"Didn't I tell you?'

Kalaiselvi frowned at him, her mouth slowly pursing like a swollen lip.

"Are you a Brahmin?" she asked.

"Why? Do I look like a Brahmin to you?"

"Is that a yes?"

Adhi got up, walked over to the boy and sat beside him. Kalaiselvi looked at his empty chair, her forefinger tapping against her lips.

"Are you though?" said Kalaiselvi. "Because it's okay if you are. It's okay if your name is really Adhinarayanan."

•

Once upon a time, Adhi had brought up the question of marriage. He wasn't sure if they would be happy, but he thought it was a good idea nonetheless. Kalaiselvi thought it was a good idea too but said no, because she had already decided to kill herself when she turned thirty-five.

"Why?" asked Adhi.

"Why not?"

"You can't say that. People aren't supposed to talk about dying like that."

"I'm not talking about killing you, I'm talking about killing me. Why do people think it's criminal to end your own life when you feel like it?"

"Because life is a gift," said Adhi. "And people with cancer don't have that choice."

"But what does that have to do with me? I don't have cancer."

"You have every reason to live."

"That's the most retarded thing I ever heard in my life."

"I don't think you're supposed to say retarded either."

Kalaiselvi dug her knuckles into Adhi's arm.

"Do you have some special reason to be alive? Are you going to be the Prime Minister of India? Are you going to eradicate poverty? What are you going to do?"

After this conversation, Adhi had gone home, taken a razor and practiced running it across his wrists. He made a series of thin red welts but could not bring himself to break the skin. He felt nauseous, then elated that life could make it so hard to die. He went to Kalaiselvi's house in the middle of the night and showed her his wrists.

"So you have a reason," she said, tracing the welts with her forefinger. Adhi watched her, looking at the first thin wisps of grey hair that were racing down the top of her head, disappearing into the brownish black tangles of her hair.

"You're really going to kill yourself," he said.

"Yes. Are you going to try and stop me?"

Adhi sighed and put his hands in his pocket.

"No," he said.

•

The late afternoon sun had made the room hot and stuffy. Tiny beads of sweat appeared on the slum boy's upper lip and forehead. He seemed to glow a little and Kalaiselvi understood, for a fraction of a second, what it was like to see a slum boy as something beautiful and small. She got up and made her way to the kitchen.

"Where are you going?" asked Adhi.

"Lime juice. You want some lime juice? It will be warm though. And not much sugar, I don't have much left."

"No sugar for me then."

"What do you mean? How can you have lime juice without sugar?"

Kalaiselvi's kitchen was cramped and smelled like a furnace so Adhi waited in the doorway. When she handed him his tumbler the juice was swirling slightly, the sediment from the sugar collecting at the bottom like speckles of salt and pepper.

"You don't want to marry me anymore, do you," she said suddenly. It wasn't a question, it was more of a statement and Adhi let it hang there, above the warm, murky tumbler of juice.

"Why not? What's your reason?" said Kalaiselvi. She drank her juice out of the mixing pot, holding it high over her mouth.

"You're selfish. Self-absorbed. And suicidal," said Adhi.

"Sssssssssssssssssssssssssssss," said Kalaiselvi.

"And you're silly."

"That's it? Those are your reasons?" Kalaiselvi rolled her eyes. He held his empty tumbler out to her and she looked at him.

"Would you like to fuck me Adhi? Would you like to have sssssssex? With someone who's sssssssssssssuicidal?"

She took the tumbler from him and wrapped one arm around his neck, her head resting on his shoulder. Adhi could see the thin, dusty legs of the slum boy in the other room. He thought they twitched for a second but he couldn't be sure.

"*En kangal rendum pallaandu paadi*," said Kalaiselvi. "Sing the rest."

"I don't know that song."

"Yes you do."

"I don't know the words."

"Don't lie. You always lie to me. You think I don't know but I do."

Adhi could feel the tumbler in her hand, gently bumping against his back.

"*Chevvaanam maalaiyil unnai thedi thedi*," said Adhi.

"See?"

Slants of thick, yellow light were pouring across the slum boy's legs. Adhi couldn't tell if they were trembling in the sunlight or whether they were lying perfectly still. He closed his eyes and heard the line *Chevvaanam maalaiyil unnai thedi thedi* play in a staticy loop inside his head. He tried to think of another song but he couldn't.

•

The slum boy was gone.

Kalaiselvi saw the empty space on the floor and laughed; then she quickly covered her mouth. Adhi stormed through the two rooms, his head turning swiftly from left and right.

"He's here somewhere," he muttered, peering out the window. He kicked the wall and strode quickly into the kitchen. Then he checked the cupboard under her sink.

"Oh please," said Kalaiselvi.

"Boys don't just disappear like that; he has to be here somewhere."

Kalaiselvi sat on the ground and listened to Adhi moving around.

"He must have snuck out. He must have woken up and jumped your fence. I thought I saw his legs move," said Adhi from the kitchen. Kalaiselvi heard things rattle and thump but she couldn't picture what he was doing. Soon he came into the front room, his face streaked with dust and sweat.

"Where are my keys, I'm going to look for him," he said. "He must still be hanging around outside somewhere. Or maybe he went home, in which case there'll be a crowd here soon, breaking down your door. I'll just see, do one round on the bike and come."

She watched him unlock the front door; then she followed him out and watched him unlock the gate.

"I'll be back in five minutes, okay? Keep the gate unlocked," he said.

Kalaiselvi nodded and watched as he started his bike.

"You can lock the door though," he said suddenly.

"What?"

"Lock the door."

"Okay."

"But keep the gate open. I'll be back in five minutes. Ten minutes."

He sped down the street in a cloud of hot, brown dust and petrol fumes. Kalaiselvi went back inside and sat down on the ground, where the boy had lain. She touched the floor and felt a thin layer of dust gently bite into the tips of her fingers. She suddenly remembered the tiny cuts around his mouth—how does a boy get cuts like that, she thought. Does he repeatedly fall face-first on sharp things? Does somebody scratch his mouth before he sleeps?

She leaned against the wall and slipped her chappals on, just to be ready. A slum mob was going to come, armed with women who would cry loudly and stick bleeding children in her face. They were going to swarm around her gate and demand she give them everything she had. I have nothing, Kalaiselvi would say and they wouldn't believe her.

The floor slowly became a long, dark smudge of gray. She leaned her head against the window, watching the fruit bats skitter across the sky as harsh fluorescent lights flickered to life in houses across the street. Kalaiselvi watched the front gate and waited.

But nobody came.

take a girl
and put her in a natural setting

Seven years later, demolition workers will find the girl's blue toothbrush. Her single room with attached bath will become a courier-travels agency before being gouged out to build a supermarket. The shelf where the toothbrush was kept will hold stacks of defective city maps and footprints made by reckless lizards. Someone will write FOLLOW ME 2 SUNAMI on the wall but this will be covered by a sticker announcing The Golden Eagle Pongal Thiruvizha.

The girl's former landlady will move to Canada. She will die of a heart attack in a 7-Eleven but it won't be mentioned in the local papers. On the day of the demolition, a young man will ignore the warnings of the workers and open a tap in the bathroom, causing the sink to fall on his foot. The blue toothbrush will be found on the windowsill and flicked onto the roof of the Public Local Call And DTP Center. A yellow cloth bag will fall from a balcony and cover it like someone closing a book.

"If You Come Today, It's Too Early. If You Come Tomorrow, It's Too Late."

firang

We break everyone like bottles, our slut hands warped and fierce like white metal bands. Then we apologize. We size our words in careful white lines, explain the stains in our teeth the bloodybaskets the bastardbitches the cowcunts. We are armed with regional anxiety. We know exactly what you're talking about.

We can laugh at our language, the bandage around our tongues that makes us othercaste, retarded, gay. Call us firang, callus firang, drag us to your TV sets and make us drink your bittersweet teas like we have always been here. Open our chests and see the runted sprays of tuberklawsis spill down like black lightning. We are all going to die from this. But you will be ok.

the flood

The flood didn't come till later. By then, the rains had stopped and the puddles were already shrinking in the sun. The ground was no longer soggy, just soft under the feet. Crushed crabs littered the road and tiny clumps of mushrooms huddled tightly in the shadows. It wasn't until the afternoon that the brown rivulets of water came racing down the road, connecting the puddles which suddenly opened up like large, glassy discs.

"Didn't I tell you?" called out the professor next door. "Big flood is coming."

The professor and his two wives were always prepared for a flood. They lived in the upper storey of their house, well stocked with candles, biscuits, bottled water, and kerosene. The professor sat on his balcony while his wives lit lamps and mosquito coils.

"You have food? Drinking water?" he asked.

"Yes," I lied, watching his wives move around him. They barely made any noise and when they did, it was like the hesitant rustling of old paper. I sat on my balcony, letting my feet get covered by swarms of mosquitos. The professor turned on his radio and made one of his wives put a mosquito coil near his chair. The road had already disappeared under a sheet of water. The people across the street were trying to make their cow climb the stairs to their roof but she had stopped halfway, unwilling to go further up and unable to go back down. When the water was already in the house and it was too late to do anything, I went downstairs. Books and papers were floating in a foot of dark brown water. I could see centipedes slowly scaling the wall—one of them fell silently into the water.

I got half a loaf of bread and two bottles of water from the kitchen and went back upstairs.

•

They were sisters. The professor had married the younger sister first and then after a year, he had married the older one. They lived quietly, going to the temple once a week, reading worn Western paperbacks in the evenings and being in a constant state of readiness for a flood. Whenever it rained, the professor would call out to me from his balcony, asking if I had food and drinking water. I would say yes, watching his wives hurry quietly around him, lighting lamps and scarring the air with the scent of kerosene. When the rain was over and the ground was starting to harden under the heat of the sun, I would watch them put everything away.

"Why are you so scared of flooding?" I asked him once.

"We're not scared," said his first wife.

That was the first time she had ever spoken to me. She never spoke to me again.

•

The next morning was filled with sunshine and the plaintive cries of the cow across the street, still stuck on the stairwell. Men with backpacks on their heads were wading through the chest-high water, selling packets of old milk for fifty rupees. The professor was listening to the radio while his wives cleaned the kerosene lamps.

"More water coming," the professor called out.

"What do you mean?"

"Two more days flooding."

Downstairs smelled like mould and stagnant water. A stray dry coconut had floated to the front door and was bumping against it, like it wanted to go outside. There were no more centipedes on the wall. I closed the windows and doors, turned off the water in the bathroom and shoved a half-empty bottle of water into my pocket. Then I went up to the balcony.

"I'm leaving," I called out to the professor. "I can't stay if there's more water coming."

"Oh I see," he said.

"You want to come? We can go slowly. We can help each other."

"No no," said the professor, waving his hand. "You carry on."

I waded through the water, feeling the rocks bite into my bare feet. A green plastic bag bumped gently passed me, followed by a small, swift snake. When I looked back I saw the professor's first wife standing behind his chair. The reflection of the sunlight turned her glasses into two shards of bright light before she turned away.

two girls

There are two girls and a boy. The boy goes missing when he is five, disappearing on a Sunday afternoon when everyone is sleeping. Two girls braid each other's hair and go door to door, asking people if they have seen their brother. They forget to show them his photograph—instead they say he talked too much, his favourite colour was yellow, and he liked eating dosa podi with bananas. Two girls do this every day until people tell them to stop being a nuisance. They watch their father grow a beard and listen to their mother cry in her sleep. Two girls learn to boil milk and make curd rice. The aunty next door invites them over for a meal and tells them that her twin sister drowned in a well when she was six years old. One girl steals the aunty's framed picture of Nehru and replaces it with a rock painted with pink nail polish. One girl leaves her a note saying "You are having smart figure I love you". Two girls watch the aunty say that they are arrogant, full of fat, and that if they ever enter her home again, she will break their teeth.

•

Two girls watch the rain with their fingers interlocked. Water backs up in the bathroom and the house begins to smell of mildew. They drink hot water with ginger and spear centipedes with their ink pens. Two girls draw kolams in their textbooks as they listen to K. Priya talk about her maama and how he puts his tongue in her mouth and squeezes her breasts. One girl asks if that hurts and K. Priya says only a little, anyway he loves me so much. One girl pictures K. Priya's maama naked and starts to laugh. Two girls go to K. Priya's house and watch porn on her maama's computer when no one is home. It's only bad when you watch alone, says K. Priya. A pixelated man drags his hand across his chest while he morosely fucks a woman from behind. One girl watches with her mouth open. One girl wonders if all men look like this when they have sex.

•

Two girls have long legs, dry brown hair laced with lice, and fungal infections that leave deep purple blooms around their crotches. Their father wears a picture of his son on a ring and gives English coaching to boys who sit in their living room, pretending not to see the two girls. Two girls memorize poems by Nissim Ezekiel and plan their future. They read news articles about girls who get raped and killed and decide that while it is generally bad to rape and kill girls, these things always happen for a reason. In the summer, their mother decides to clear out the almirah and throw away anything that hasn't been used in the past six months. They find dead lizards, a framed picture of Nehru, and two pairs of small, blue shorts. Two girls put these things in a plastic bag and promise to burn them in the back. Each girl keeps one pair of shorts. One girl keeps the framed picture of Nehru.

•

Two girls get a wedding invitation from K. Priya and notice that she is not getting married to her maama. They eat watermelon in the summer and make alternative plans for the future, which include computer classes and weekly trips to Melmaruvathur. One girl thinks they will get married to wealthy brothers who own a lorry company. One girl thinks no one will marry them and they will develop terminal diseases in their breasts. Their father puts a photograph of his son on the television and their mother dusts it every day with the end of her sari. Two girls look at it and think that the boy looks poor, angry and nothing like their brother. Two girls look for photographs of two girls. But they can't find any.

anarch

"In China They Do It with Chillies" is a racist song, but it's okay for you to sing it in India because there are hardly any Chinese people here. Your favourite line is "And fuck knows for what". You like the way everyone leans forward and spits out the word "fuck". You believe it means something profound and sad when they sing it that way.

You look at The Young Man In The Blue Shirt. He is walking in front of you, shouting "In China they do it with CHILLIES. Chillies, machan, fucking red chillies, shove it right up their—" he claps and nearly loses his balance. Yesterday you tried to tell him what it was like to carry a cello home in the snow. You told him how you easily made the transition from two braids to ponytail but getting your parents to let you wear your hair loose was a different matter altogether.

You tried to explain why Anne of Green Gables is so important to Canadians and why at some point, almost every girl and some boys wish they could run around Prince Edward Island wearing ugly dresses. The Young Man In The Blue Shirt frowned and said what's a green gable? You shoved him in the chest because you know he hates this. You said he was retarded.

"In Mumbai they do it with MIRCHIS," bawls The Young Man In The Blue Shirt. Kanna, who is walking beside you, immediately starts shaking his head.

"China machan," he says. "It's China."

"Fuck you. This is India. We are all Indians. We do it with mirchis," says The Young Man In The Blue Shirt.

"Yes but it's all about China," says Kanna.

"In China they do it with CHILLIES," bellows The Young Man In The Blue Shirt, grabbing you by the waist.

"And FUCK knows for what," you say, even though that line doesn't come yet.

•

When I grow up, I'm going to be an angel.

This is officially the stupidest thing you have ever said in your life. You said this in front of everyone in second grade, right after a boy called Jeff said he wanted to be a pastor like his dad. When your parents hear of this, they become upset because they think you want to be a Christian. They consider home schooling. They consider sending you to India. For the next five years, you live in perpetual fear that they will pack you off in the middle of the night and you will have to live in a hut and shit at the side of a dirt road because there are no bathrooms in India. You start drawing pictures of mutilated angels on the back of your binder. On the front of your binder you write things like PANTERA 4EVER, METALLICA RULZ and I LUV SEBASTIAN BACH. In the library, you start cutting out glossy pictures of angels and hiding their heads, wings and torsos in different *Choose Your Own Adventure* books. Someone tells on you and you are fined. As an afterthought, you are assigned a counsellor. You think this is awesome but ask them not to tell your parents because they might send you to India and India really scares you. They tell your parents anyway.

•

The song of your life comes from a Kannada movie called *Operation Diamond Racket* that was released in 1978. You are particularly fond of the chorus that goes "If You Come Today, It's Too Early. If You Come Tomorrow, It's Too Late." These lines mean different things to you at different times. You sing it under your breath when you wait for people. When you are very happy, this song makes you upset. When you are upset, this song reminds you of running through sprinklers in the summer with a best friend you don't have anymore.

Sometimes when you are drunk, you call The Young Man In The Blue Shirt in the middle of the night to tell him he is retarded.

He says, *If you come today—*

It's too early, you say.

If you come tomorrow, he says.

It's too laaaaate, you say.

You pick the time, he says. *Tick Tick Tick Tick Tick Tick.* And then? What comes next, he says.

You say *Darling* and he says what? He keeps saying what and you keep saying *Darling.*

Later, you try to teach this song to some people at a party but they end up singing "In China They Do It with Chillies" instead.

•

At school dances, no boy will dance with you. You are thankful for this because your parents would totally ship you off to India if they ever found out you were dancing with a boy. Indian parents are psycho like that. You say this to anyone who happens to be standing next to you.

In eighth grade during Social Studies, a girl called Adrian sits beside you when the class watches videos about Brazil. She smells like watermelon bubble gum. You are suddenly aware of your ribcage and how the bones in your hips stick out. You can feel the hair growing on your upper lip. You wish you were a boy. You think you would be better at everything if you were a boy. You secretly touch the ends of Adrian's dirty blonde hair and think of having sex with girls. You think of having sex with boys. The Brazil video ends and you think of going home and killing yourself. You think of drinking an entire bottle of Dettol. You think of beating yourself to death with a snow shovel, even though it would probably hurt a lot.

•

At 4 A.M., young men have a contest to see who can say your name five times fast. They do tequila shots between each round and shout "Otha Mayire" each time someone gets it wrong. Everyone messes up your name on the first or second try and this makes you feel powerful and hopeless at the same time. You are sitting beside Kanna, who is bored and wanted to leave two hours ago. You ask him if it is easier to be gay in America. He rolls his eyes and says can we go now and you say no.

At 4:15 A.M., young men have a contest to see who can say your name backwards. The Young Man In The Blue Shirt stands up and says he can say your name five times fast backwards. He can say it standing on one leg. He can say it with his eyes shut. Watch, he says. He closes his eyes and you hold your breath. Then he shouts "In China they do it with CHILLIES!"

You tell yourself you knew this would happen.

•

When you are 13, you are assigned two counsellors because nobody knows what to do with you. You think this is cool and tell them you are suicidal so they don't lose interest in you. Whenever they ask how you are, you say you are depressed. You tell them that you give yourself eraser burns on your thighs. You also tell them you are a Satanist though you're not sure what this means.

You write Anarchy Angel on your binder in permanent black marker but you spell "Angel" wrong so it says Anarchy Angle and you can't wash it off. People want to know what the Anarchy Angle is. They ask to see your wrists and you say you are into pills. You say you have boyfriends who live on the other side of town who wear safety pins in their ears and beat up their stepfathers. No one believes you.

On a Sunday when you are practicing your cello, you get a phone call saying your friend Anjali has hung herself with a belt but she isn't dead yet, she is in a coma. Your father says if she wakes up, she will have brain damage. You ask if this means she will be retarded and your father says not to use that word in his house. During the funeral, you decide that Anjali was retarded. You think her funeral is retarded and the fact that everyone is crying is retarded. The next time someone calls you a Paki, you pummel them in the face with your binder, releasing surprisingly large amounts of blood. When you get in trouble for this, you point out that while you repeatedly used the term motherfucking asshole, you didn't call anyone retarded, not even once.

•

Kanna decides he wants a tattoo. He decides you also want a tattoo but first, you both take the bus to Pondy Bazaar to look at the pavement stalls and think about the permanency of tattoos. While looking at piles of colourful ten-rupee underwear, you decide to go for it and quickly catch an auto before you change your minds. You meet a mechanic called John who gives you both village tattoos for 200 bucks. Kanna gets the word "Dasi" done on the back of his neck, which makes John laugh. You think it would be a good idea to get "Anarchy Angel" tattooed across your wrist but it is so painful you make John stop even though he's only written "Anarch". Kanna feels this is all his fault. To make up for it, he takes you to see *Titanic* dubbed in Tamil in a shabby theatre that is almost empty. Halfway through the movie, you notice Kanna is crying and you think this is because of the tattoo. You're such a fag, you say. At some point, Kanna disappears. You call The Young Man In The Blue Shirt and he picks you up. He wants to know if "Anarch" is some Canadian thing.

"It was supposed to say 'Anarchy Angel'," you say.

"Anarchy Angel," he says. "Oooooh."

"Fuck you," you say.

"You could have just got 'Angel', no? Unless 'Anarch' is some Canadian thing I don't know about."

You don't think about Kanna until the next afternoon, when he calls to say that he tried to kill himself by taking sleeping pills and he just woke up and now he feels really stupid. You think this is an extreme thing to do and tell him it's just a tattoo. He starts to sob and says fuck oh fuck over and over again. He says how stupid is that? You try to kill yourself and you wake up! How fucking stupid is that?

You tell him no, he is not stupid.

The Young Man In The Blue Shirt grabs the phone and says yes, he is stupid. People who try to kill themselves are stupid people.

You tell Kanna not to mind the Young Man In The Blue Shirt because he is retarded. We are all retarded you say and Kanna starts to cry again.

•

You are on the bus home after a junior high dance. Sitting in the next seat is a girl called Heather who you were good friends with in elementary school but she won't talk to you in junior high. Because you are on the bus and it is practically empty, she tells you how a ninth grader called Mathew tongued her during the dance. She doesn't need to tell you because you saw it happen. This was the first time you saw someone French in real life and you were surprised at how awkward it looked. My tongue feels weird, says Heather.

You get off at the next stop, even though it's still four stops away from your house. When you get home your mom is angry because it's late and there was a call from the school saying that you were taking an interest in Satanism and suicide.

Satanism, Hinduism, same thing, you say and your mother slaps you. You think you are going to cry but you don't.

•

You lose.

You are sent to an all-girls college in India and this ruins any chances you have of becoming a single mother and living in an apartment with someone called Ryan or Darren. You get love letters from girls who are enamoured by the way you dress and your accent. They say they like your figure and your smile. You keep these letters safely and look at them from time to time to make sure they are still there.

There are no counsellors here. The "disturbed" girls roam around the campus, stay at home, sit in the library or wait in the car park. They are not allowed to loiter in the canteen or look out the window during class. The ones who wear long sleeves are the ones that cut themselves. You real-ize that you can sit in class completely stoned and people will just think you're sleepy. Nobody carries binders or advertises the fact that they listen to Pantera. Angels aren't a big deal here.

Whenever there is a group dance event, you get cast as a man along with all the sports girls. This is because you are not graceful but you are tall, quick and you smile easily when you move. Your partner is a Jain girl called Pooja who you usually don't notice because all Jain girls look the same to you. But when you start dancing, she always looks straight into your eyes and she mouths the words of the song like she wants to fight you. When she sings the words "Bichua Jawani Ka" she tilts her head and arches her eyebrow and you forget your steps. You think the song is about girls that are mesmerising and poisonous. After the college farewell party, Pooja hugs you and whispers something in your ear in Hindi which you don't understand.

You tell this to Kanna when you are both sitting in front of a tea stall, eating violently orange bajjis. Ever notice how Jain girls get really fat after they get married, he says. You nod and he tosses the rest of his bajji to a stray dog.

•

The Young Man In The Blue Shirt is wearing a black t-shirt that is covered with tiny holes in the back. You are both in the hospital because Kanna has finally overdosed on sleeping pills but he is not dead. If he lives, he will feel stupid and try again later. If he dies, he will have accomplished what he set out to do and you think this is a good thing even though you don't say this out loud.

You look at the word "Anarch" tattooed on your wrist. Every time someone asks you what Anarch means, you tell them something different. Anarch is an Inuit word that means struggle within the heart. Anarch is Old Tamil—it means an absence or negation of everything. Anarch is Arabic—it is a term of endearment used among homosexual men. Someone tells you that Anarch is an actual word that has something to do with anarchists. You are secretly pleased by this but say you're not interested in what it really means. Every time someone asks why you don't get it removed, you tell them to go fuck themselves. Sometimes you say this in Tamil, without actually using the word fuck. Sometimes you say this in English using fuck multiple times.

The Young Man In The Blue Shirt is singing "In China They Do It With Chillies" in a soft voice so it doesn't wake the elderly couple that have fallen asleep in the next seat. You're not sure why they are here but they have two wire baskets filled with food. They offered you idlies which you refused but The Young Man In The Blue Shirt accepted and said were very nice. They think you are married and you are flattered that anyone would think you were marriageable.

"In China they do it with chillies," says The Young Man In The Blue Shirt, his hand tapping gently on your arm.

"And fuck knows for what," you say.

about the author

Kuzhali Manickavel was born in Winnipeg and currently lives in Bangalore. This is her second collection of short stories. She used to blog at thirdworldghettovampire.blogspot.com.